"That was...wow!" Chris said. "Want to do it again?"

Alyssa laughed then rolled over to look at his face. "Hell, yes. You?"

"Absolutely." He kissed her hard. "But I need a moment to recharge."

"Television?"

"Seems appropriate," he said, grappling for the remote.

"Don't even think you get to be in charge of that thing," she said. "We are not watching sports after sex."

"Sports after sex is a time-honored tradition," he insisted. "Like a cigarette."

"I don't smoke," she said, leaning across him. "So give me the remote."

"Try and get it," he said, scooting away from her. Then he stopped. "Wait a minute. See, this is how it starts. First sex. Then a power struggle for the remote. We're well on our way to coupledom."

Coupledom.

The word echoed in Alyssa's head, killing her smile. This was supposed to be only a fling, not a relationship. But how was she supposed to let Chris in on that secret?

Blaze™

Dear Reader,

Happy holidays from the Southwest!

I love the holiday season—the sparkle of the lights, the decorations in the stores and the laughter and romance that always seems to be wafting in the air as much as the scent of cider and roasting turkey.

And, of course, what better time to fall in love?

Unless, of course, you're a girl with no guy on the horizon.

Fortunately, Chris is there to help her out. Her best friend for ages, Chris is desperate to take their relationship to the next level. So when he thinks that Alyssa's got her eye on another man, well, Chris knows it's time to pull out all the stops and either seduce the woman he loves or lose her forever.

I hope you enjoy Chris and Alyssa's story.

Happy reading,

Julie

P.S. Alyssa's friend Claire has a story, too: a New Year's romance. *Moonstruck,* coming in January!

USA TODAY Bestselling Author

Julie Kenner

STARSTRUCK

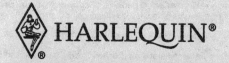

HARLEQUIN®

TORONTO • NEW YORK • LONDON
AMSTERDAM • PARIS • SYDNEY • HAMBURG
STOCKHOLM • ATHENS • TOKYO • MILAN • MADRID
PRAGUE • WARSAW • BUDAPEST • AUCKLAND

Recycling programs
for this product may
not exist in your area.

ISBN-13: 978-0-373-79512-3

STARSTRUCK

This edition published by arrangement with Harlequin Books S.A.

® and TM are trademarks of the publisher. Trademarks indicated with
® are registered in the United States Patent and Trademark Office, the
Canadian Trade Marks Office and in other countries.

www.eHarlequin.com

Printed in U.S.A.

ABOUT THE AUTHOR

Julie Kenner has always loved stories—reading them, watching them on television and on the silver screen, and making them up herself. She studied film before attending law school, but knew that her real vocation lay in writing the kind of books she loves to read. She lives in Texas with her husband, two daughters and several cats.

Books by Julie Kenner

HARLEQUIN BLAZE
 16—L.A. CONFIDENTIAL
 98—SILENT DESIRES
194—NIGHT MOVES
269—THE PERFECT SCORE

Don't miss any of our special offers. Write to us at the following address for information on our newest releases.

Harlequin Reader Service
U.S.: 3010 Walden Ave., P.O. Box 1325, Buffalo, NY 14269
Canadian: P.O. Box 609, Fort Erie, Ont. L2A 5X3

The Starr Resort in this story is a completely fictional place, but the location (and a few amenities) is loosely based on the fabulous Bishop's Lodge Ranch Resort & Spa, of which I have fond memories.

Super special thanks to Brenda Chin, Kathleen O'Reilly and Jess Dawson.

1

Clip-clop, clip-clop, clip-clop.

Prince Robert lifted his head and whinnied, to the delight of all six people riding in the horse-drawn carriage.

In the back row, Alyssa Chambers snuggled under the blanket, a cup of warm cider held tightly in her hand. The soft strains of Bing Crosby crooning "Winter Wonderland" drifted back from the speakers hidden low on the carriage side walls. Colored holiday lights sparkled in the fog, the mist giving them an ethereal quality that seemed appropriate for the Christmas season.

The carriage moved steadily down the street, providing Alyssa and the other passengers a stunning view of the ornate homes in Dallas's Highland Park neighborhood, now shining and sparkling for the holidays.

"Oh, man," Claire Daniels moaned. "Isn't this just the most romantic night ever?"

Beside her, Alyssa turned, brows raised. "Um, hello? Dateless, remember?"

Claire lifted her chin. "I'm practicing the power of positive thinking."

Alyssa glanced at the two rows in front of them. Two rows with four people. Two couples. Two guys. Two girls. And they were snuggled under blankets, arms around each other, oblivious to the lights, the music—everything but each other.

And Alyssa, well aware that she was enjoying a romantic carriage ride with her best friend instead of a *boy*friend, swallowed hard on the jealousy that rose in her throat.

"Positive thinking, huh?" she asked. "Is it working?" If it was, she was going to have to try it—really try it. Because despite all the ho-ho-ho and happy-holiday festivities that Dallas offered up during late December, Alyssa wasn't feeling the seasonal love.

"Not in the least," admitted Claire. She'd broken up with her boyfriend a few months prior. Or, rather, he'd broken up with her. And the loss of Joe had hit Claire where it counted—her pride.

Alyssa frowned, her mind whirring as she sat quietly in the carriage, plotting creative ways to torture the idiot who had decided that Christmas events should be designed for couples.

Party hosts expected you to arrive with a date. The theater sold dinner-and-show packages for two. Even the carriage ride to see the famous Highland Park lights seated you in even numbers, as if you weren't anybody unless you were part of a pair.

Was it any wonder the suicide rate increased during the holidays?

Alyssa had been single since summer, when she'd

broken up once and for all with her boyfriend Bob. It had been a particularly unpleasant breakup, since they'd started out as friends. Good friends. Solid. But after a while, they'd started dancing around the attraction thing, and before Alyssa knew it they were out on a date, and then they were in bed and then they were a couple staring down the road of life to marriage and kids and a dog.

At first, that had seemed perfect. But then little things started to get in the way, and soon, neither Alyssa nor Bob could even remember why they'd been friends. They seemed so uniquely *unright* for each other that even the memory of the times they used to just hang together had been tarnished.

The breakup had been worse because it had been two breakups: one with the lover and one with the friend. And as an added injustice, Alyssa had been dateless ever since.

"At least you can take Chris," Claire said. "To all the parties and stuff, I mean."

Alyssa nodded. Chris was a prime example of not making the same mistake twice. Her across-the-hall neighbor was desperately sexy, funny and easy to talk to. But he was her friend, and had been from the get-go. The stamp of friendship was firmly on his forehead, and despite the fact that he was sweet and smart and incredibly hot, there was no way she would ever risk that friendship for sex. No way, no how.

She'd learned *that* lesson with Bob, in a big way.

Not that sex was even in the realm of possibilities.

When she'd first met Chris, she'd felt a warm tingle of attraction, and then firmly and soundly squashed it. For one thing, the tingle had so clearly *not* been reciprocated. In the two years they'd known each other, he'd never made even the slightest hint of a move on her.

At first, Alyssa's pride had been tweaked by his failure to come on to her, because that was what guys did, right? And, yeah, also because the tingle she'd felt had been more like a loud, clanging bell. But the truth was that his disinterest made her life easier, because Chris, with his freelance-writer lifestyle, was squarely N.M.M.—*Not Marriage Material*. Alyssa had never seen the point in dating guys who didn't even land on the possibility spectrum. Yes, she'd broken her rule on a few occasions and gone out with guys who were clearly not the matrimonial kind, but she'd never managed to stay friends with them after the inevitable breakup. Better to put those kind of guys in the Friends column from the start and avoid any messy entanglements later.

As far as she was concerned, Chris was at the very top of that column. And, yeah, there were times late at night—when they were watching a movie or making margaritas—that she'd feel a warm flood of desire and frantically wish he'd do something to make that scarlet N.M.M. disappear. But she knew better than to believe that would ever happen. She'd grown up with a man just like Chris, after all: a freelance writer out perpetually chasing a story—and a paycheck.

Alyssa could remember the long weeks when her

dad was away on writing assignments, and the pang of longing for a father who was never home. She'd beg to go with him, and when he returned, she'd pore over the pictures and imagine that she'd been right by his side. But her dad never took her. Not feasible, he'd said. Not when she had school and he had to work.

He'd tell her and her mom that he had to chase the stories so that he could pay the bills, but Alyssa had overheard the frequent arguments about money, and most particularly about the fact that her father had turned down an offer of full-time employment at the local paper.

McCarthy Chambers's wanderlust kept him from holding a steady job, and even though he claimed he'd be the next Truman Capote—and was constantly at work on some never-published epic tome—he never managed to land the big stories, much less the big paychecks. When Alyssa's mom was laid off from her teaching job, the family not only lost their car, they lost their home, and eleven-year-old Alyssa found herself living in a one-bedroom apartment with paper-thin walls instead of a charming little house on a tree-lined street with her best friend two doors down.

She'd hated her father that month, an emotion that had been even harder to handle because she loved him so desperately. When he was around and life flowed smoothly, he was a joy. But when money was tight or he got sucked into a creative vortex, it had been a black, lonely hell.

And now that his various medical issues had forced

Alyssa's dad to stop traveling for work, her parents
were struggling to make ends meet with their minimal
Social Security checks. *Not* the life Alyssa wanted. Not
at all.

As an adult, she figured she understood now what
made her dad tick. Intellectually, she could acknowledge that he was a man who had wanted a nomadic life,
and even though he'd loved his wife and daughter, he
should never have been a family man.

Alyssa loved him, she understood him, and she'd
even forgiven him for the crappy chunks of her childhood. But there was no way in hell she was ending up
like her mother. No way she was foisting that lifestyle
on her own children. Alyssa Chambers had very specific
things she looked for in a man, and financial responsibility and a steady presence in the house were tops on
that list.

And Chris—who didn't even have a savings account
much less health insurance, and who spent weeks
bouncing around the globe writing travel articles—was
definitely not that man. Not in a big way. Even as "just
friends," his devil-may-care attitude drove Alyssa nuts.
He was an exceptional writer, and had a great relationship with *Tourist and Travel*, one of the premier travel
magazines in the world. From what Alyssa had seen,
Chris could have easily landed enough articles to earn
him a solid annual salary. But instead, he worked only
when his money was running out, and then he'd take
anywhere from three to five assignments back-to-back
and disappear for two months. The rest of the time, he

holed up in his apartment working on a series of novels that he was hoping to sell.

Alyssa told herself that she admired his creative spirit, but the truth was she didn't know how he could stand it. She'd forced him to have The Money Talk once, and he'd admitted that he banked his writing checks, lived off them until the well ran dry, then took another gig to fill the pot back up again. He didn't carry insurance on his motorcycle, and he'd actually lived a few months on beans, rice and spaghetti because he'd purposely turned down an assignment in order to stay home and work on his book.

It wasn't even her life and she was stressed just thinking about it.

Bottom line? There was no way—*no* way—a guy like Chris would ever end up on her love life radar. Which meant that though she might have an escort for holiday parties, she didn't have a *date*.

As the two sets of couples in front of Alyssa and Claire snuggled closer—completely oblivious to the fact that they were rudely thrusting their public displays of affection all over the less fortunate in the carriage—Prince Robert turned to the left, then started down yet another austere, tree-lined street. Like all the houses in Highland Park, these tended to be homes to old-money families, the elite of Dallas society. The kind of people who still participated in debutante balls and who could trace their lineage back to the days when Texas was a republic. The kind of people who either stayed home, or took the whole family with them when they traveled.

"That one," Claire said, pointing to an utterly traditional colonial-style mansion. "That's always been my favorite in this neighborhood. And look! The topiaries are shaped like Santa's elves!"

Alyssa had to concede the topiary point, but the house itself did nothing for her. It was big, but it didn't have personality. Even so, given the chance, she'd live there in a heartbeat. The house, she knew, belonged to Russell Starr. And Russell Starr was M.M. all the way. Not even the slightest hint of an *N* in sight.

The Starr family was Texas royalty, and a century ago had founded the eponymous Starr Hotels and Resorts, a luxurious worldwide chain that had faltered seven years ago after Thomas Starr had passed away, leaving the future of both the company and the family in the hands of his then twenty-three-year-old son, Russell.

Because Alyssa had gone to school with Russell, she'd paid attention when the business community had rumbled about the massive hotel chain being left in the control of an inexperienced twenty-something upstart. And while the society mavens and business naysayers had forecast doom and despair for the company, Alyssa had believed that Russell would pull the family business out of its slow spiral toward oblivion. And she'd been right. Now, seven years since Russell had taken the helm, the Starr chain of resorts was bigger than ever, with hotels on four continents, five-star ratings across the board, and a guest list that would make even the most jaded celebrity watchers drool.

"I'm hoping to land him," she said. "Well, Starr Industries."

"Really?"

"That's my ambitious plan," Alyssa admitted, though she, so far, hadn't thought about how she would implement that plan. But she needed to soon, because although her billable hours were outstanding and she'd brought in an exceptional book of business over the course of the year, she hadn't brought any clients to Prescott and Bayne this quarter, which meant that as far as the partners were concerned, she was the ugly stepchild compared to Roland Devries, who was the other associate with his eye on the partnership slot.

The partners were meeting right after the holidays to decide who would be invited to join the firm as a junior partner, and unless Alyssa could rectify that deficiency, she was afraid that Roland would get the job for which she'd worked so hard. And *that* was simply not acceptable. She'd gone into law school planning on making partner by the time she was thirty, and she'd signed with Prescott both because of the firm's stellar rep and its fast track to partnership. Like being a tenured professor, partnership in a law firm meant job security and income stability, and for Alyssa, that was the Holy Grail.

"Do you think you have a shot? I mean, surely he's got attorneys coming out of his ears."

"Actually, the company handles most of their legal work in house."

"And you're thinking he'll hire your firm because…?"

"Remember that fundraiser for Love without Boundaries I worked on earlier this year? The gala and auction to raise money for medical care for orphans in China? Russell was on the committee, too, and he mentioned that he was considering retaining an outside firm so that his in-house staff could focus on big-picture issues and function more in a supervisory capacity." She shrugged. "So why not Prescott and Bayne?"

"Why not, indeed," Claire said, eyeing her suspiciously. "A guy like Russell Starr's probably courted by a lot of firms. Why you?"

"For one thing, Prescott's got a great reputation."

"So does Daniels and Taylor," Claire said, referring to the firm her grandfather had founded. "So do lots of firms."

"True," Alyssa conceded. "But we talked about it, and I really got the feeling that he would be open to me sitting him down and explaining why he should choose Prescott."

"So why isn't he already with the firm?"

Alyssa could feel her cheeks warm. "I was planning to make an appointment after the gala wrapped, but by then…well…I felt a little awkward about it."

Claire's eyes narrowed with suspicion. "Why?"

Alyssa drew in a breath. "Because he kissed me. The night of the gala."

"No way. Seriously?"

"Depends. Is one hot-and-heavy kiss within your definition of serious?"

Claire turned to face her dead-on, her jaw hanging open. "Why didn't I know this?"

Alyssa shrugged. "I was still dating Bob. It just happened, you know? And I felt terrible afterwards."

"Details," Claire demanded. "Right here. Right now."

"Honestly, there's not a lot to tell," Alyssa said, feeling so under the microscope she was almost sorry she brought it up.

"The hell there isn't. Start at the beginning." She waved a hand. "Go on."

Alyssa sighed, trapped. "The truth is, we went to high school together, so I've known him for ages."

Claire's brows lifted. "You went to school with Russell Starr?"

"I'm pretty sure his family actually endowed my scholarship." Her gaze darted again to the Starr property, and she sighed. A family like that didn't have to scramble for a paycheck or worry about making partner.

"Were you guys friends?"

Alyssa shook her head. "Not back then. He was a grade ahead, but he was every girl's fantasy guy, you know? The guy in school that you're certain would be absolutely perfect if only he'd notice you."

"Well, duh. Starr family. How much more perfect can you get? But, hello? When are we getting to the kissing part? What happened? Tell me everything. He asked you out on a date?"

"Sort of. My car had a flat, and he drove me home."

She shrugged. "On the way, he suggested we stop for drinks."

Alyssa still thought that was a key piece of information: they'd stopped at *his* suggestion.

The night had been fabulous, full of wine and laughter and even a few long, heated looks, and it had only gotten better when he'd delivered her straight to her door. She'd invited him in, but he'd declined. What he'd done instead was lean in, tell her he'd had a wonderful time, and kiss her oh-so-gently, but with a ton of promise. She'd felt the tingle all the way down to her toes as he'd walked away. And she'd stood like an idiot in front of her apartment door as he'd walked back to his car and driven away.

Bob had come over for breakfast the next morning, and Alyssa's Cinderella delusions had evaporated. After all, Russell was a society-page regular, and at the time, she'd still been happily dating Bob. The drink had been a drink, and the kiss a sweet memory. Nothing more.

Still, she could fantasize. And regularly did, for that matter. Her thoughts drifting to what would have happened if he'd come inside for that kiss. Who knew where it might have led...?

She sighed, her breath clouding in the chilly night air.

"Wow," Claire said. "Talk about the one that got away."

Alyssa rolled her eyes. "I never had him in the first place," she said. "He can't get away if I never had him."

"A fact about which I hope you are soundly kicking yourself. He kissed you good-night and you never even followed up? Called him again? Made any move to let him know you were interested?"

"I was with Bob," Alyssa said, her voice small because she knew Claire was going to jump all over that.

"And you *told* him that?"

"Claire, I was *dating* him. We were serious. Or I thought we were. Yeah. I mentioned him."

Now it was Claire's turn to roll her eyes. "Never mention to a guy that you're dating another guy. All guys need to be kept in the realm of possible until you're married. That's a simple fact of life." Alyssa scowled, but Claire barreled on. "So what happened after you and Bob broke up? With Russell, I mean?"

"What happened? Nothing happened."

"You didn't call him? I mean, forget the whole legal-retainer stuff, but didn't you at least *call* and ask him out for drinks?"

"No! Of course not."

Claire shook her head as if Alyssa had utterly failed. "You know, if it wasn't for Joe being an absolute prick and you being completely clueless, we could be double-dating tonight instead of escorting each other."

Alyssa sighed, knowing that Claire was absolutely right.

She glanced around, taking in the dancing lights of the Highland Parks neighborhood. The children going from door to door singing Christmas carols. The couples strolling the neighborhood, their faces close as they shared kisses under mistletoe.

Romance was in the air tonight. It just wasn't in the backseat of the carriage.

2

"DROP THE KNIFE."

"*I don't think so.*" Max Dalton held the small pocket-knife steady as he stared down the barrel of Eli Whitacker's Glock 9mm. Not exactly an ideal situation. He'd broken into the abandoned warehouse hoping to find a clue as to where Whitacker might have stashed the girl, but he'd never expected to find Whitacker himself.

Max never considered that he might not walk out of the warehouse at all. That things weren't going exactly as planned was an understatement, to say the least.

"I said," Eli repeated, "drop the knife."

Max tried to calculate his odds, came up with a depressingly low probability of success, and let the blade clatter to the concrete floor.

"Good boy. And now if you'd be good enough to get down on your knees."

"I don't think so."

Eli's grin widened. "No problem. You can die just as well standing up."

Eli's finger moved, gently squeezing the trigger

that would, at any moment, fire a shot of lead into Max's gut.

He did the only thing he could do, even though it was futile and useless—he tried to dive to the left.

And as he did, his eardrums burst as a shot rang out. He flinched automatically, anticipating the pain of the bullet connecting with soft flesh.

But there was no pain. Just Eli standing there, a red stain spreading out on his chest, and a blood bubble forming at his mouth.

Eli fell to his knees, revealing the woman behind him, a gun held tight in her shaking hands.

Her.

Dark hair that fell in soft curves to brush against her shoulders. A square jaw and dancing green eyes. Long dancer's legs that he could imagine wrapped tightly around him.

He saw her, and he wanted. Craved. Needed.

She was his fantasy. His inspiration. His complete and total distraction.

"Alyssa," he heard himself whisper. "Alyssa, you're alive."

CHRISTOPHER HYDE stared at the computer screen, frowned, then methodically backspaced over the last bit of text he'd written, changing *Alyssa* to *Alicia*.

He shook his head. Still too close, what with the letter *A*. He backspaced again, and suddenly the femme fatale's name in his second Max Dalton novel became Natalia.

Better.

Better still if he would go in and change the description, but he couldn't quite bring himself to do that. Maybe once the whole book was finished he'd change her hair from black to red. Right now, though, he could only see the girl in his imagination. Alyssa-called-Natalia.

And, yeah, she was the girl of his dreams.

He'd started writing the Max Dalton series before he'd met Alyssa. The character had been in his head for years—an obscenely wealthy freelance operative who traveled the world on assignment for the highest bidder. Max had Chris's own wanderlust, and although Chris had never rescued a child kidnapped by terrorists or scaled a mountain range trying to find ancient artifacts before the bad guys located them, he poured his own fantasies into the character. His childhood had been staid, boring. He'd seen nothing other than his small Texas hometown, population 712, until he was twenty years old. But he'd read every *National Geographic* that came in the mail cover to cover, and he'd fantasized about seeing those places himself. About having adventures all over the world.

His journalism degree had been his ticket out, and now he earned his keep by traveling the globe and writing about it for tourists. And with any luck, one day he'd supplement that income with royalties from the Max Dalton novels he was currently trying to sell.

He'd landed an agent with the first book, and she was about to begin pitching it to publishers. The entire

process was nerve-wracking, and he was trying to
bury the nervousness by burying himself in the second
Max Dalton adventure. An adventure in which Max
teamed up with another operative—a female—who
may or may not be an ally, and who was most definitely
a lover.

And who in his head was all Alyssa.

Chris still remembered the day she'd moved in.
She'd been trying to drag a battered, butt-ugly recliner
from her rental truck to her apartment. He'd offered
either to help her carry it or torch it, her choice. She'd
gawked at him for a long second, and at first he'd feared
he'd gone too far. Then she'd collapsed into the recliner,
bent over with peals of laughter. The chair was a gift
from her father, she'd said. "He has terrible taste, and
he never should have spent the money on the damn
thing, but I love him." She shrugged. "So it'll get a
place of honor in the living room."

The next day, she'd knocked on his door, and invited
him over to see how she'd "done up that hideous chair."
He'd walked inside, then breathed deeply of the smell
of cinnamon and cloves that seemed to fill her apartment, a scent that now belonged entirely to Alyssa,
prompting delicious thoughts of her at random times
and locations. Especially now, during the holiday
season.

As for the chair, it was tucked into a corner next to
an absolutely hideous gold-plated floor lamp decorated
with flying cupids. She'd hung a velvet painting of
dogs playing poker behind the chair, and set off the

entire area with a small gold shag rug that looked like a reject from an Austin Powers movie set. The corner was in utter contrast to the rest of the living room, with its soft lines and feminine colors.

"I'm calling it the corner of testosterone," she said, and he could see her lips twitch with suppressed laughter.

"I think my testosterone is offended," he'd said dryly. She'd stared for a moment, and then her laugh had burst forth. "Seriously, though, I like it."

And that combination—that subtly sexy girl who was willing to be a little bit silly because she loved her dad—completely swept Chris off his feet.

Not that he'd told Alyssa that. Alyssa knew he was alive, of course, but she thought of him as a friend, not a flesh-and-blood man. A sad state of affairs for which he had no one to blame but himself.

At first, she'd been dating some guy—Bob, Bill, something—who had never been good enough for Alyssa. And Chris didn't put the moves on attached women, no matter how sexy they were.

But even when that happy day had come and she'd kicked Bob to the curb, Chris still hadn't made a move. Hadn't even hinted how he felt.

She'd come to him, told him about the breakup, and suggested they watch something fast-paced and mindless on his big-screen television.

He couldn't say no, of course, and though she'd seemed fascinated by the car chases and explosions, he'd spent the movie wondering how to tell the woman who'd become one of his best friends that he'd fallen hard and fast for her. And then, when the movie had ended, she'd smiled at him with sad eyes and reached for his hands. There'd been a window of opportunity right then. A single short window during which he could have done what Max Dalton would have so smoothly done—leaned in and kissed her. Told her in no uncertain terms that he wanted to be more than friends.

But while Chris might write Max Dalton, that didn't mean he walked the walk. Especially not where women were concerned. A sad reality that was cemented when she'd said, "Thanks for letting me hang out with you. I really need a solid friend right now."

He'd swallowed. Her words had felt much the way he imagined a knife to the heart felt like. Sharp and painful and totally deadly.

He knew then he had no chance with this woman. Not as a rebound guy. Not as anything.

It was, he'd thought, one hell of a crappy wake-up call.

Still, he needed to do something. More and more, she was on his mind. Creeping into his dreams. Into his books. Hell, Max Dalton was not a one-woman kind of guy. He got in, he got out, he did the job, and he blew shit up. He didn't turn all gooey for a girl.

Except lately, he did. And Chris had a feeling that unless he got Alyssa out of his system, Max Dalton was going to turn into a one-woman man, and then where would Chris be? Probably writing a romance novel instead of the second testosterone-laden spy thriller he'd told his agent was in the works.

Max Dalton wouldn't let thoughts of a woman torment him like that. He'd just sidle up to her, whisper in her ear and take her to bed.

A nice fantasy, but that's all it was. A fantasy.

Chris wanted more. Warmth and reality and lazing around in bed with the paper on Sunday morning. Shoving jeans and T-shirts into backpacks and taking off for Paris on the spur of the moment. Hiking along a beach at sunset, especially a white-sand beach in some exotic location.

And damned if he didn't want that with Alyssa.

Frustrated with himself, Chris got up from his desk and stretched, his eyes wandering to his door as he did so. He needed to get his ass in gear and start packing. He had to catch a flight first thing in the morning.

The phone rang, and though he considered ignoring it, he knew he had to answer. Technically, he was already on assignment, and if it was Greg, his editor at *Tourist and Travel,* then Chris really did have to take the call.

Caller ID showed only a New York area code, and he snatched it up, expecting Greg and instead hearing the harsh, cigarette-soaked voice of Lilian Ashbury, the powerhouse agent Chris still couldn't believe he'd landed.

"How fast can you finish the second Max Dalton book and get me an outline for the third?" she asked without preamble.

"Happy holidays to you, too, Lil."

"Bah humbug. It's slush and ice up here, not a damn thing to be happy about."

"Is that why you're working on a Saturday?"

"I'm tireless in my efforts to represent you," she said, deadpan. "I had lunch with Roger Eckhard," she said, referring to a senior editor at Main Street Books, Chris's dream publisher. "I pitched him the book, and he loves the concept. He's leaving on the fifth to start the New Year with two weeks in Italy, and I want him to take both manuscripts and an outline for the third with him. We want him looking at this series like a franchise, and you as the next Ian Fleming. If he does, I think we can expect the kind of offer that will make you a very happy man."

"I—"

"Just say 'Thank you, Lil.' And 'No problem, Lil.'"

"No problem, Lil," he said, fighting a grin. He'd make it work. No sense telling his agent that the proximity of his next door neighbor was keeping his head in a decidedly un-Max-like mode. But that was okay. Because he was about to go spend a week in New Mexico in a flashy, splashy resort. He'd shift between writing the article for *Tourist and Travel* and writing pages of Max Dalton's next installment. He'd hole himself up in his hotel room, crank out the pages, and produce some fabulous shit.

With over six hundred miles between him and Alyssa, how hard could it be?

3

"GEORGE BAILEY, I'LL love you 'til the day I die."

"Awww." Alyssa sank down into her overstuffed sofa and dabbed her eyes with a tissue.

Claire tossed a handful of popcorn at her. "The movie's barely even started."

"I know," Alyssa said with a sniffle. "But I know what's going to happen." She sniffed again, then blew her nose. "It just gets me every time."

"And the alcohol's probably not helping."

"You're the one who insisted on peppermint schnapps and hot chocolate."

Alyssa couldn't argue with that. And, hey, the libations had done their job. They'd both come home from the carriage ride in a funk. The original plan had been to pick out a handful of the many invitations they'd both received and go party-hopping, hoping they'd slide gracefully into the holiday spirit.

But after they'd climbed into Claire's car, neither one had the energy, and they'd ended up at Alyssa's apartment, trying to drown their depression in schnapps-laced hot chocolate and a hefty dose of Frank Capra.

"Why can't we be like Mary Hatch and get a guy like George Bailey?" Alyssa asked.

Claire lifted a brow. "You don't want a guy like George Bailey. He wants to travel and never has money to fix up his house."

"It's a movie, Claire," Alyssa said, even though her friend was absolutely right.

"You want Sam Wainwright," Claire said, exhibiting perfect understanding. "The hardcore businessman to George Bailey's laid-back guy."

"Alas, there are no Sam Wainwrights in Dallas."

"Russell Starr," Claire said, then sat back looking proud of herself.

"What about him?"

"Not two hours ago you told me he was your fantasy man."

"So?"

"So do something about it."

Alyssa gaped. "You are seriously crazy, you know that, right? We went out for drinks. One kiss—"

"An amazing kiss."

"—but just a kiss," Alyssa said. "It's not a great romance, Claire."

"Of course not, since you didn't call him the next day and push for an actual date."

No, Alyssa had to admit, she hadn't. And that was something for which she was still kicking herself. He'd known about Bob, of course, and so she could totally justify in her mind why *he* hadn't called *her*. She was taken. And it was that same reason that had prevented *her* from calling *him*. Considering she'd broken up with Bob only a few months later, perhaps she should have rethought that decision.

"You need to learn to go after what you want, Al," Claire said, frowning as she concentrated on her words. Their mugs were filled with more mint than chocolate, and it was clearly going to their heads. "If there were sparks with Russell that night, you should go for it."

"The only thing I'm going to go after right now is that partnership. If I don't bring new business to the firm in the next couple of weeks, my chance takes a nosedive. I already know that Bayne is gunning for the slot to go to Roland. He wants a new partner with SEC experience. He figures that since Prescott's specialty is mediation, that makes me extraneous."

Although Alyssa had a number of clients for whom she did general litigation work, more and more she was taking on mediation jobs, setting herself up as an arbiter of disputes and trying to help the sides negotiate their way to a settlement and avoid the financial and emotional toll of a trial. She loved the work, believed in its value, and it irritated her that Roland got partner points simply because he focused on securities law.

Still, she couldn't ignore reality, and if partnership at Prescott was off the table, that meant that she'd have to start looking for a new job, because she wasn't about to stay at a firm that was a dead end. The idea of job-hunting gave her hives, and she took another sip of minty chocolate to dull the pain caused by the mere potential.

"Who says you can't do both?" Claire said, lifting her brows. "A little business…a little pleasure…"

"Claire!"

"Don't you at least owe it to yourself to try?"

"Fine. Maybe. I will concede that Russell Starr would be a great catch. But he's taken. The man's dating a United States senator's daughter."

"Not anymore." Claire took a sip from her mug, her eyes dancing. When the mug came away, a chocolate mustache highlighted her upper lip. "Broke up last week. Your boy's single."

"Oh." The schnapps in Alyssa's stomach started doing a Riverdance kind of number. "You're certain?" She didn't really have to ask, though. As the daughter of a Texas state senator herself, Claire always had the political/social gossip at her fingertips.

"Interesting little tidbit, huh?"

Alyssa frowned, wondering if it even mattered. She had no idea how to go after a man like Russell. And while she enjoyed a fantasy as much as the next girl, the odds that he would come after her were slim. He was the kind of guy who dated celebrities and public figures. Not really in her league.

She took another sip and squinted at her friend, who was holding a finger out and looking downright serious. "What?" Alyssa asked.

Claire frowned, confused. "I was going to say something, but I can't remember what. But it was profound. Trust me. Profound and brilliant, and if I could remember it right now, it would be the key—the absolute key—to both of us finding the perfect man and living happily ever after."

"Christmas is only five days away. Can't Santa just drop the happily-ever-after in our laps?"

"What would you tell him to drop?" Claire asked, sitting up straighter. "Seriously. Give me five things. Five things that would make this your most perfect Christmas ever."

"Partnership. Locked in."

"Boring much? Come on, give me something a little more interesting. This is the holidays. The season of parties and fine frockery."

"Frockery?"

"You know. Dresses and stuff."

"I am so cutting you off from the schnapps."

"Just tell me. Come on. You know you want to. Come on," Claire said, her voice low and urging, as though she was trying to coax a reluctant tabby cat into a carrier. "Come on. Tell Claire every little thing."

"Fine! All right! Russell Starr," Alyssa said. "Russell Starr *would* make it a perfect Christmas." What the hell? This was fantasy, right? And he was gorgeous. He was stability and security personified. He was fun to be around. And he could land her a job-saving client.

"Better," Claire said, setting her mug down before she sloshed more chocolate. "But I want more. Christmas isn't just about getting the guy. What would make the holiday really perfect for you? Five things."

Alyssa frowned, trying to think something up. But the truth was, everything else about the holiday was going along pretty well. "Good friends," she said, aiming a winning smile at Claire. "How about you?"

Claire's grin turned wicked. "Good friends."

"Cheater. You stole that one from me. What else."

"I haven't got a clue. Can we drop the list down to two?"

"That depends," Alyssa said magnanimously. "What's the second?"

"The perfect guy."

Alyssa tossed a pillow at her. "Didn't I start out there?"

"So let's do something about it. You need to call Russell."

"I am calling, remember? Client. Partnership."

"A date, Alyssa. You need to call him for a date."

"I don't know—"

"He kissed you. Trust me. The Russell ball is firmly in your court."

"Yeah, but—"

"But nothing," Claire said firmly. "Santa's elves don't deliver men. You want a relationship, you have to go after it, balls to the wall."

"That's your plan, too?" Alyssa asked, wanting to deflect attention. "Who's your guy? Joe? Or is he on your shit list?"

"He won't be on that list anymore if he comes back to me, right?"

"Claire…" Alyssa couldn't help it. She'd never liked Joe. Not something she could tell her best friend, though. Not when he and Claire had been so serious.

And not when there was nothing specific for Alyssa to point to. He was just…something.

And *something* wasn't sufficient to justify disclosure. Because the last thing Alyssa wanted was to confess to her friend that she didn't care for her boyfriend, and then find out that Claire and Joe had gotten engaged.

"Then it's settled," Claire said firmly. "We have a plan."

Alyssa shook her head. "I don't think I can—"

"Yes," Claire said firmly, "you can. Who's the girl who told Bob she'd had enough?"

"I did," Alyssa said, her stomach already twisting into knots. "But that was like making the decision to give my bicycle to Goodwill. You're asking me to commit to buying a Rolls Royce."

"You deserve a Rolls," Claire said. "Why shouldn't you have one? And you wouldn't be buying it, anyway. Just test-driving. But how will you know until you go take it for a spin?"

"I think this analogy's getting out of control."

"Maybe," Claire conceded. "But you have to work for your own happiness, and doesn't that make sense even more during the Christmas season?"

"I do work for my own happiness," Alyssa said. "Law school. Job. Really good paycheck." Even as she said it, though, Alyssa knew that wasn't enough. The working world wasn't a safe place. Her mom had been a teacher for fifteen years when she'd gotten laid off without any warning at all. And lately Alyssa was getting calls from law-school friends who'd lost their jobs when the economy had done a number on their firms.

Besides, she didn't want to be a single girl forever. Not even a single girl with a bank account. The one thing her parents had always had—even despite the fights about money—was love. Her dad may have been Mr. Irresponsible, but he loved her mom deeply and passionately, and her mom returned it in spades. Alyssa wanted that. Craved it. A home. A family.

She just didn't want the drama that her mother had put up with, and she wanted to know that the mortgage would always get paid.

"You know I'm right," Claire said, watching her shrewdly. "So let's go out and get what we want. Take the bull by the horns. The man by the—"

"Claire!"

"Well, you know."

Alyssa drew in a breath. She'd had a fabulous time with Russell that night they'd had drinks. They'd laughed and talked, and there'd been not a single awkward moment. And then it had all fizzled away.

Why on earth had she let it fizzle away?

"Maybe you're right," she said, taking a breath for courage. "It's our holiday, our lives."

"And *our* men." Claire smiled, smug and determined. "We just have to make them realize it." She reached for her mug, then held it up in a toast. "To making this the best holiday ever, and to starting the New Year with our men at our sides."

Alyssa thought of Russell. Of the way he'd smiled at her when they were working on the fundraising campaign. The way his eyes had darkened when she'd drawn a maraschino cherry into her mouth. The way they'd laughed over nothing in particular.

And the way he'd kissed her ever-so-gentlemanly when he'd escorted her to the door that evening. And then she imagined his hands on her in a very not-so-gentleman-like way....

Yeah, she thought as she clinked her mug against Claire's. *I can drink to that.*

ALYSSA STARED at the Web page. Russell wasn't even in Dallas at the moment, which meant that not only was Claire's Go-for-the-Guy plan not happening, but Alyssa's own plan to meet with Russell and try to wrangle a new client for the firm had been shot all to hell.

Instead of being conveniently located downtown, Russell was in Santa Fe, at the gala opening of the Santa Fe Starr, an over-the-top, total luxury, full-service, five-star resort located about twenty miles outside of Santa Fe proper. According to the articles she'd found, the resort was absolutely state-of-the-art and the height of luxury. The guest list for the week surrounding Christmas Day was chock-full of the rich and famous, including a few Oscar nominees and Emmy-award winners. All proceeds from the first week went to Love without Boundaries, the charity that Alyssa knew Russell supported wholeheartedly.

"You have to go there," Claire said.

"Are you crazy? It's invitation only. It says so right there," she added, pointing to the article.

"You *have* to go," Claire repeated. "You have the entire week off, Alyssa. This is the perfect time. Besides, we just made a Christmas pledge. You can't wait until after the season to follow through on a Christmas pledge."

"I didn't know the pledge would involve cross-country travel," Alyssa said, thinking of the plane that would inevitably be involved.

"One state. New Mexico's right next door."

"Claire." Alyssa injected a hint of warning into her voice.

"I'm serious. This is your chance."

"What? To make a fool of myself?"

"To find out if there's anything between you and Russell. He asked *you* out, remember? You should have followed through back then. You didn't. But now you have a second chance. So don't blow it."

Alyssa licked her lips, unsure. Russell was perfect, and exactly the kind of man she knew she wanted. But still—

"It's also your chance to nail partnership."

Now *that* was Claire talking sense.

"That's your cover for going to the resort," Claire continued, as if Alyssa weren't already on the same page. "The reason you tell Russell you came. To talk about what Starr Industries wants in its outside legal counsel. You need a new client, right? What better chance to line one up than when you're looking all sexy and gorgeous in a black slinky dress?"

"And it makes sense to talk to him away from the office," Alyssa said. "Remind him that we go way back. Maybe even grab a meal with him so that we can get more into the details of what Prescott and Bayne can offer than we could during a half-hour slot in his office with the next appointment scratching at the door."

"All the experts say that if you want to land a client you first make them a friend." Claire grinned. "Sounds to me like you're well on the way with Russell."

Alyssa shook her head. "But mixing business and pleasure. It could get awkward…"

Claire rolled her eyes. "Jumping the gun much? You don't have the client or the boyfriend yet. Just *go*. See what happens. You owe it to yourself to follow up on this, and you damn well know it."

Alyssa licked her lips. "I'm not sure if it's crazy or brilliant."

"Brilliant," Claire confirmed, passing Alyssa the phone even as she picked up her own cell phone and pushed a speed-dial number. "Dial."

Alyssa did, calling information first, and then getting patched through to the hotel's front desk.

"I'm sorry. There simply are no rooms. The resort is in holiday previews, and the rooms not already booked by the public have been blocked off for the guests of the Gala Opening."

"Oh! Right! Well, that's me. I'm coming to the gala."

Across the room, Claire lifted her brows.

"Name, please."

Alyssa hesitated, wondering how she was going to

pull this off. Since nothing came to mind, she said her real name and hoped she could fake it. "Chambers. Alyssa Chambers."

There was tapping as the woman on the other end of the line checked a computer. "I'm sorry, Ms. Chambers. You don't seem to be on the guest list. Perhaps you should contact the Starr corporate offices and see if there's been an error?" Though the woman was perfectly polite, Alyssa could hear the accusation. *Perhaps you should hang up now, you lying little twit.* "Shall I connect you directly?"

"Yeah. That would be great. Oh." She pretended that she'd just thought of something key. "Once we get the gala invitation thing straightened out, will I have a room? Or will I be back here with you, trying to find a place to sleep?"

"All the gala invitees have rooms preassigned."

"Great. Thanks."

Hold music hummed, and just as someone was picking up with "Starr Industries, how may I help you?" Alyssa hung up the phone.

Basically, she was screwed. No rooms at the hotel unless she was an invited guest, and no way to become an invited guest.

"Maybe you should call Russell and ask for a ticket?"

Alyssa gaped at Claire. "Are you nuts? Even if his secretary puts me through, how am I supposed to explain? 'Gee, Russell, I want to invite myself to the gala so I can hit you up for your business?'"

"Not work," Claire said. "Romance."

"Like that's much better. 'Hey, Russell. I had such a great time having a drink with you that one night, please arrange me a room in Santa Fe.' Um, no."

Claire made a face. "Okay, you have a point." She stood up and hooked her purse over her arm.

"Wait a second. Where are you going?"

"Drinks," Claire said. "Joe. He's going to pick me up." She held up her cell phone. "My side of the pledge is moving forward just fine."

"But—"

"You'll get there. I have absolute faith."

Alyssa watched her friend go, wishing she had Claire's certainty. Because at the moment, the only way she could think of to get to that gala was to ask Russell for a ticket. But that was hardly the image that she wanted of her in Russell's head. He needed to think of her as competent and capable. A woman who could represent his legal interests and slide easily into his life. She wanted him smitten on absolutely every level.

And one didn't reach smitten by begging for a room.

No, she'd get to the resort on her own. Or not at all.

Unfortunately, *not at all* was looking more and more likely.

Maybe she should book a room at a nearby motel and then wander over to the Starr Resort for the evening festivities.

A quick look on the Internet put the kibosh on that plan, though, as it was clear that privacy had been one of Russell's primary concerns in designing the resort.

It wasn't close to anything. And with the predicted snow and the winding roads, Alyssa had no intention of driving from a Motel 6 to the resort on a daily basis.

Damn.

There had to be a way.

Except there wasn't.

She sat back on the couch, the mug cupped in her hands, her entire being shifting into mope-mode. Probably best to accept the reality that saving her job and getting the guy was idiotic and oh-so-unlikely.

Sometimes reality really was a bitch.

She sighed, took another sip of chocolate, and decided that it was time to forget about crazy fantasies and force herself into getting some holiday spirit. From the corner of her apartment, the small Christmas tree she'd bought seemed to beckon. She'd held off decorating it, because despite the lights and the carols and the parties and the wassail, the season didn't feel like Christmas. Not when she was sitting there, a dateless wonder.

"Pathetic." With a sigh, she dragged a chair to her hall closet, her head spinning slightly from the schnapps and lack of dinner. Her apartment was ancient and had great— if poorly designed—closet space. The hallway linen closet was designed in two sections, with the main section being reachable by normal people, and the top section being accessible only by giants. Add to that the fact that the space went back several feet, and Alyssa sometimes wondered why she hadn't bought a full-blown ladder to keep in the apartment so that she could get to all her stuff.

Balancing on the chair, she yanked open the cabinet, then pulled down the giant plastic bags stuffed full of summer clothes. Behind them, she'd stashed the boxes of Christmas ornaments, and now she stood on her toes, trying to get her fingers to connect with the boxes.

Just a teensy bit closer...

Her fingers brushed the cardboard, but she couldn't get a grip on the smooth box. *Dammit.* She knew there was a reason she should've hung on to that ugly step stool she'd hauled to Goodwill last month. Now what was she going to do?

With no other options, she climbed off the chair, grabbed a broom from the pantry, and climbed back on, this time armed. She shoved the broom into the abyss, eased it between the box and the wall, and started using it to ooch the box forward. The box, however, was not inclined to cooperate, and so she jerked hard on the broom, punctuating the move with a rather loud, rather definitive curse.

The box moved.

Not only did it move, it shot forward, having apparently been blocked by a slight bump in the wood that Alyssa's persistent shoving had overcome.

It teetered at the edge of the closet, Alyssa's fingers keeping subtle pressure so it didn't fall, every ounce of her concentration going to keeping her balance despite the mushiness that was her head. She took a breath, satisfied that all she had to do now was shift a little and close her fingers around the box.

But when she tried, the box—that same box with her

grandmother's delicate glass ornaments—tilted forward at a dangerous angle.

She could picture the box sliding through her hands, crashing to the ground, and the ornaments her grandmother had passed on to her smashing into so many bits of colored glass.

Who knew that decorating a tree under the influence could be so dangerous?

She tried to edge the box back into the closet, figuring she could borrow a proper ladder from the manager and try again, but the box was having none of that. Instead, it seemed, her destiny was to remain right there, balanced on a chair, her hands above her head getting tired as she kept a box from falling. And there she would remain until she passed out from hunger or her arms atrophied for lack of blood.

Three taps sounded at the door, and the wave of relief that crashed through her was so intense it almost had her sagging—and the box dropping. "Chris! Come on in!"

The doorknob rattled, and even as she remembered that she'd locked the door, she heard his frustrated "It's locked, Alyssa."

The box teetered, she tilted back to catch it, her head swam and she yelped. "Chris!"

"Hang on!" he called.

She heard the slam of his own apartment door, followed a few seconds later by the rattle of a key in her lock. She said a silent thank-you that she'd designated both Chris and Claire as the keepers of her spares, and then muttered a desperate "help!" as the door burst open.

"What on earth—"

She heard the confusion in his voice contemporaneously with his footsteps pounding across her apartment. She couldn't turn her head to look, but she didn't have to. She felt his hands around her waist, holding her tight, and the simple pressure gave her such a sense of security that she wanted to cry. She wasn't going to fall backwards and break her neck. She wasn't going to drop her grandmother's heirloom ornaments.

Chris had arrived, and everything was going to work out just fine.

"What were you thinking?" His arm shifted, and she realized he was in short sleeves. The bare flesh of his arm brushed against her midriff, exposed now because raising her arms had raised the pajama tank top above the waistband of her Sylvester and Tweety pajama pants. For a moment—the briefest of moments—she felt a sensual thrill whip through her. Her nipples peaked, and her breath hitched, and she cursed Claire for all her talk about boyfriends and holiday romance because right then all those old Chris-lust thoughts that she'd so thoroughly quashed came rushing back.

At first, she'd ignored that sensual tingle because she'd been dating Bob when Chris had wandered into her life. Then, she'd tamped it even more firmly down because she'd learned about his frequent travel schedule and utter disinterest in managing his money or his career.

Best just to be friends, she'd told herself, and that had been easy advice to follow when she was dating Bob. Now, though, she was single, and even if Chris was as N.M.M. as they came, she couldn't stop the heat—*the desire*—that was bubbling up inside her.

She told herself it was the schnapps. *The. Schnapps.*

Because this was *Chris*. Her friend. Her *best* friend besides Claire, and she was not in a million years going to let herself get the hots for him. She treasured the friendship too much to let holiday cheer and an innocent touch blow everything good there was between them.

But, oh, my gosh, she'd like to feel the heat of his kiss right about then.

"Alyssa!"

"What? What?" She realized he'd been talking to her. She'd been in a sensual funk, and she'd completely spaced out. "What did you say?"

"I said, how heavy is the box?"

"Oh. Not very."

"Then let go."

"No way! It's full of Christmas ornaments. The thin glass kind. No way I'm letting them shatter. Why do you think I'm teetering on my toes in the first place?"

The hand on her abdomen shifted, and Alyssa stifled a moan. Alcohol and skin-on-skin touches really didn't mix. Not if she wanted to keep her wits. Not to mention her distance.

"Do you trust me?" he asked, his voice thick and rich, like warm, delicious chocolate.

"I—" She cleared her throat, mortified that talking

was so difficult. The drink, she thought, and the fact that she was currently in the midst of a major romantic dry spell. But she had a plan, and a goal, and a Starr on the horizon. And she *would* focus. "I do. I trust you."

"Then let go of the box."

She took a deep breath and pulled her fingers away, moving to grab the door even as he broke contact with her, his own hands going up to catch the box as it fell.

"Got it. Now let me get you."

She looked over her shoulder to see that the box was safe and sound on the floor, and when she turned back to face the closet, she felt Chris's hands on her bare waist. "Turn around," he said.

"No, I—"

"Turn."

She turned, and he lifted her off the stool even as he pulled her closer to himself, then slowly eased her down until her feet were touching the floor. It was a sensual journey, and though she imagined that the elapsed time could probably be measured in seconds, to her it seemed like hours. Lazy, hedonistic hours with the press of Chris's hard body against hers, and the glancing thrill that accompanied the way her breasts brushed softly over his chest as he lowered her body in front of his.

Once her feet were on the ground, she tilted her head back to tell him thank you, and suddenly his mouth was right there, the corners curved up in a grin that was both sexy and cocky, and she realized that she wanted to taste those lips more than she wanted to breathe. And even though a reasonable, rational Alyssa screamed that she was about to make a huge mistake, the Alyssa in Chris's arms shut her ears and raised herself onto her toes, and then closed her mouth over his and took exactly what she wanted.

4

FOR ABOUT two seconds, Chris was certain that he'd not only died, but had landed squarely in heaven. The second after that, his brain processed the fact that Alyssa—his Alyssa—had pressed her mouth hard against his, her arms tight behind his head as if she wanted to deepen the kiss.

Chris was a lot of things, but he wasn't an idiot, and he opened his mouth, giving her access, then swallowing a low guttural groan as her tongue swept inside, hot and demanding.

She tasted of chocolate and mint, and though he had absolutely no idea what had gotten into her, he saw the kiss as a challenge—a chance to prove he was worthy of this woman who every day filled his thoughts and fantasies.

Chris had always loved a challenge, and he met her lips with gusto. His tongue warred with hers, his mouth claiming her, sucking and nipping on her lower lip even as his hands splayed across her back, holding her closer to him, the contact setting every inch of his body on fire.

She wore a thin pajama top, and her body rubbed against him, her nipples like hard pebbles against his chest. He wanted to touch, to explore, to memorize every inch of her body, but he didn't, terrified that at the slightest wrong touch she'd pull away and this magical bubble would burst.

Part of him wanted to risk it, though. To take his cue from Max Dalton, who wouldn't leave his hands on her waist. He'd slide them up, skimming under the skimpy top, his fingers on her back, his thumbs easing forward to stroke the curve of her breast.

He wouldn't stop there, either. He'd present a full assault, sliding his thumbs forward until the pads teased her nipples, then deepening his exploration of her mouth as his hand slid down to the waistband of her flimsy pants. He'd feel every twitch of her skin, every sweet hesitation, but she wouldn't tell him to stop, and that simple surrender would arouse him as much as the feel of her body against his.

He'd slip his hand down, his erection painful with need, then moan when his finger found damp curls and her slit, already wet and ready. Only a little bit more, and he would brush her clit and she would tremble in his arms, her back arching, and her lips parting beneath his mouth as she whispered one sweet, simple word: *Yes.*

No.

The real world rushed back to smack Chris in the ass. "What?" he said, groggy and confused.

"No," Alyssa repeated. "I'm sorry." She backed

away from him, managing to look both completely turned on and utterly mortified.

"I'm so sorry," she repeated. "I should never have— I'm just…I'm just sorry."

"It's okay," he said, though it wasn't at all. His body was on fire, his desperation acute. He wanted her back in his arms. He wanted to finish what they'd started, and then he wanted to go from there.

But in truth they'd barely started anything. The woman who'd melted under his touch had been only in his fantasy, and the woman he desired so desperately was now standing in front of him regretting a single kiss that had passed between them.

And that, thought Chris, was a damn shame.

"I'M SORRY," she said again, but Alyssa was certain she needed to keep repeating that in order to make it real. Because at the moment, she didn't feel sorry at all. She felt incredibly turned on, and that really wasn't good.

She turned away, scrubbing her face in her hands. "I mean, that was really beyond the pale, wasn't it?" She'd *kissed* him.

And good Lord, but that had been one hell of a kiss. Soft, yet firm. Demanding, yet sweet. The kind of kiss that not only soaked a girl's panties, but had her thinking about pink roses and hand-holding.

Dear God, what had she been thinking? Not only did she *not* want to go there with Chris, but he had never once given her any hint that he was remotely interested in her.

Or, rather, he'd never given her any hint before five minutes ago. Because from the way he'd kissed her back...from the way his hands had stroked her...the way he'd felt, all hot and hard as he'd pressed up against her...either he was a very good actor, or there was some definite interest going on there.

And though she told herself there was absolutely no way she would repeat that kiss or go any further whatsoever, her own body was calling her out as a liar. Her damp panties. The way her skin seemed to tingle like someone standing next to fifty thousand volts of raw electricity. And her nipples, now hard as rocks under her thin pajama top. *Not* good. Definitely not good.

Since she really couldn't have a conversation with him about how that kiss was a mistake if her body was screaming otherwise, she ducked into the bathroom for a robe to toss on over her pajamas, then came out hoping she looked cool and collected. "I...um...I've been drinking schnapps."

"Ah," he said, as if that explained everything.

"It's just that Claire was here earlier, and we were drinking and talking about sex and—" She stopped. Her rambling was definitely not improving things.

"Anyway, I, um, totally stepped out of line and I'm really sorry and really embarrassed and—"

"Alyssa," he said, an obvious smile in his voice. "It's okay. I get it."

She pretty much sagged in relief. "Really? It's just— the schnapps, and—"

"Seriously. I get it."

"Right. Of course." *Of course* he got it. He was probably as mortified as she was. He was a guy, though, so was it any wonder his body had sprung to attention? He was probably happy to push the whole thing behind them fast, fast, fast.

He waved toward the hall closet. "So what exactly were you doing?" He turned before she could answer and moved into her kitchen. She heard the water running, and by the time she arrived behind him, she saw that he'd splashed water on his face and was patting himself dry with a towel.

"I've got cocoa in the slow cooker," she said, wishing a million times over that she could erase this sudden awkwardness between him.

"Sounds good." He knew her kitchen as well as she did, and grabbed a holiday mug for himself, then fixed cocoa with just a splash of schnapps. "How about you? A refill?"

"I don't know," she said wryly. "Schnapps seems to be dangerous to me."

As she'd hoped, he laughed. But what she hadn't expected was the heat in his eyes when he said, "I've never run from danger."

"Chris…"

He held his hands up. "Just lightening the moment."

"Sorry. I'm still edgy." She ran her fingers through her hair. This was *Chris*. As good a friend as Claire. She should not be feeling all awkward and weird around him. "Too much holiday cheer. Not to mention holiday sugar." She squinted at him. "And it's late. Why did you come over here, anyway? It's Saturday, shouldn't you have a hot date like the rest of the human race except me?"

"Working," he said.

She perked up. "Are you doing another article? You were complaining last month that you were going to run out of rent money early next year and—"

"I'm cool," he said. "And yeah, I have another job in the pipe. But I've been working on the next Max Dalton book."

"Oh."

He laughed. "Tell me how you really feel, Alyssa."

She could feel her cheeks heat. "I love your book, you know I do," she said, meaning every word. "But wouldn't it make more sense to cram in a few more articles? Really pad your bank account?"

"Your concern for my well-being is overwhelming," he said with a lazy grin. "But if I worked all the time, when would I play?"

She rolled her eyes. "You don't play. You either work for money or you work for free. I just think you should—"

"Work for money. I know." He shrugged. "Hopefully I am. My agent seems really encouraged."

"Yeah? That's awesome."

"But?" he asked, his tone so teasing she almost rolled her eyes.

"Fine. Fine." She held up her hands in self-defense. "Pretty soon you'll tell me I sound like your mother, so I'm dropping it. But I have two words before I do."

"Good times?" he teased.

"Retirement plan," she said.

He nodded. "Don't worry. Got it covered."

And since she was quite certain that he didn't, she decided that was her cue to drop the subject. In truth, his work ethic impressed her. She knew he was perpetually broke, of course, but at least he knew what he wanted, and he threw himself after it wholeheartedly. She just wished he was a little smarter about the whole thing. Or at least smarter than her dad had been. Because her parents were heading into retirement with little more than dust in their IRAs, and while Alyssa would do what she could to help them out, she'd hardly reached the point where she was made of money, and she was desperately afraid that her childhood would be repeated in their old age, and they'd lose the house that they'd bought during her senior year of high school.

Maybe Chris really would play it smarter. She had friends from law school who weren't half as dedicated as he was, and she'd been impressed with the way he'd worked his tail off to finish that book. She'd even admired the fact that he'd been willing to sacrifice so much to do it, although she still didn't understand how he could stand to live without some sort of monetary cushion.

Still, his tenacity was something to be emulated, and right then and there she decided she'd follow his example, channel her inner Chris, and pursue Russell and Starr Industries with equal tenacity.

She aimed a smile at Chris, then lifted her mug in a toast. "To you," she said.

His brows lifted. "Really? Just like that? No lecture on holing myself up? No Q and A on the state of my bank account?" He moved toward her, his eyes dancing. "I subject myself to your whims. Interrogate at your will."

Her whims.

She swallowed, her mind playing tricks on her and making his words lascivious and seductive where surely he'd only intended them to be teasing. Feeling antsy, she turned away, ostensibly fiddling with an ornament hanger. When she had the little wire hook firmly in place, she looked up at him. "My grandmother bought this one for my mom's first Christmas," she said, holding up the antique Santa. "She collected them."

"I know. You told me about her once. Her first was a glass Christmas tree."

"You're right," she said. "I'm impressed you can remember such trivia."

"Well." He shrugged, but didn't meet her eyes. "Anyway, I should get going. The truth is that I was hoping you'd help support me in my gainful pursuit of a paycheck."

"Huh?"

He grinned. "I was hoping you'd bring my mail in. That article I said I was writing? I'm taking off tomorrow morning. Can you feed Horatio and Charles?" he asked, referring to the two giant goldfish that he'd bought the week she'd moved in. He'd paid a grand total of forty-nine cents, including tax, and the fish had started their life in a wineglass. Neither Chris nor Alyssa had expected them to live, but live they did, and they grew, too. Each time Chris moved them to a bigger bowl, they just kept on growing. Soon, Alyssa thought, they'd need an apartment of their own.

"No problem," she said, removing a delicate glass Santa from a nest of tissue. "Travel magazine have you covering some fabulous holiday destination?"

"Actually, yes."

She looked up, frowning. "But the December issue's already on the stands."

"A new resort. So I'm writing an article about the hotel, the amenities, the location. The full-meal deal. And since the grand opening is over Christmas, they've also got me writing an article for the magazine's Website and doing a daily blog entry."

"Yeah? I'll have to read it. Can I cyber-heckle you?"

"I'm counting on it," he said, with the kind of soft smile that had her grinning back in easy familiarity.

"Overseas?" Most of his assignments were out of the country and involved writing about fabulous vacation spots, and despite the fact that Alyssa hated flying, that part of his job made her green with envy. Especially since in the last three years, the bulk of her travel for work had been to such exotic destinations as Texarkana and Brownsville. Not exactly Paris or Tokyo.

"Stateside," he said. "I'm happy I won't be jet-lagged over the holiday, although I'm bummed not to be home for Christmas."

"You won't be here?" She looked up at him, a little

band tightening around her heart as she realized how much she'd been anticipating spending Christmas morning with him. "I was going to cook and everything. I mean, since I'm not going to Austin to see my parents this year."

Her mom and dad were traveling to Kansas to see relatives, and Alyssa had actually been looking forward to spending the holiday at home for the first time in years. But part of what she'd been looking forward to was spending it with Chris and Claire.

"Sorry. I don't come back until Saturday. I'm going to miss you, too. I was looking forward to burned turkey and dry dressing."

She threw a wad of tissue paper at him. "Oh? Were you planning on cooking? Because I know you aren't dissing *my* culinary skills."

"Wouldn't dream of it," he said, then cleared his throat. "That reminds me. Since I won't be here on Christmas, I brought your present. I thought you could open it now. If you want. Since I'm going away."

"Really?" She felt ten pounds lighter, and told herself the delight came with the season and with presents. It was a generic thrill, not specific to any one giver. "I haven't gotten you anything. Yet," she added. The truth was that she'd been looking for a present that seemed Chris-ish for the past three weeks. Nothing, however, rang true, and she was beginning to get a little irritated with herself. Even shopping for Claire hadn't been so trying.

"You don't have to get me anything," he said, retrieving a small box from where he'd set it on a table.

She followed him to the couch, then settled herself beside him. Her fingers were itching to take the present, but she pretended she was sitting on her hands, and waited for him to pass her the box. "It's nothing much," he said, putting the festively wrapped gift in her hands. "But I saw it and remembered your grandmother's ornament collection, and, well…"

He trailed off, and she looked up at him, delighted. "This is so sweet. Thanks. Really." The box was wrapped in gold paper with a shiny red ribbon. At first, she thought a store had wrapped it, but then she saw the tell-tale signs of the personal touch—rough-cut edges, tape that shows through, and a knot in the bow that only an amateur could have managed.

The realization that he'd wrapped it himself made her feel all sappy.

"Go on," he urged. "My grandmother doesn't take this long to open presents."

"Sorry." She tore into the wrapping to reveal a white box, and when she lifted the lid, there, nestled among a snowy mound of fluffy cotton, was a green glass Christmas tree with a gold star on top and *Lone Star Christmas* etched along the bottom. She drew in a breath and pulled it out, dangling it from her finger by the delicate gold cord. "Chris, it's beautiful." The work, actually, was fantastic. A lot of glass ornaments were now factory made, but this one had a certain delicacy about it that suggested it was hand-crafted.

"I found it at the Armadillo Bazaar in Austin," he said, confirming her suspicions that it was handmade.

Without thinking, she leaned over and hugged him, then pressed a soft kiss to his cheek. "I love it," she murmured, only too late realizing how stiff he'd gone inside her hug, and how tense his jaw was under her lips. Quickly, she backed away, realizing her mistake. Twice in one night she'd come on to a guy who wasn't interested. Worse, she reminded herself, she'd come on to a guy whom she wasn't interested in. Could she be any more lame? "Seriously," she said, this time keeping her exuberance limited to her voice. "It's great."

"I'm glad." He'd pulled a pillow into his lap, and now he drummed his fingers on it, as if he suddenly had realized that he needed to get out of there. Alyssa wanted to kick herself. Honestly, she was never, *ever,* drinking schnapps again.

"Um, if you need to go… I mean, you must have packing to do."

"No," he said immediately. "I'm good."

As he made no move—to leave or otherwise—she cleared her throat, then got up and hung the ornament he'd given her in a place of honor on the tree. "Looks great, doesn't it?"

"Absolutely," he said, but when she turned to smile at him, he wasn't looking at the tree, but at her.

She shifted her weight from one foot to the other, suddenly uncomfortable under his inspection. She turned back to the tree and dragged up more conversation. "Ah, um, so where are you going? Someplace snowy and Christmasy?"

"Actually, yeah," he said, shifting the pillow away as he reached for his mug again. "The hotel that's opening is in Santa Fe. Pretty snazzy stuff, actually. If I weren't so stressed out about finishing the second Max Dalton book and an outline while I work on the article, the situation would be beyond perfect."

"Finishing?" she asked, looking back over her shoulder in time to catch his pleased smile.

"Lil called about an hour ago. Apparently she thinks we have a real shot at selling the series."

She squealed and caught herself before she actually jumped into his arms, and the fact that she wasn't there, sharing a hug to celebrate his good news, sat as wrongly with her as her early desperate groping had. "That's amazing," she said, which was nothing short of a huge understatement.

"I'm not holding my breath. A shot isn't worth anything unless we hit the bull's-eye."

"You will!" she said. "The book's awesome." She'd read the first one and loved it. The hero was witty and sexy and utterly dangerous. She could see little bits of Chris in the Max Dalton character, and it had been such fun imagining her easygoing friend writing about a hard-ass, mega spy.

"The atmosphere will be right, anyway," he said. "There's at least one formal event, and Dalton always—"

"Wait." She pressed her fingertips to her throat, where her pulse was beating wildly. Because all of a sudden the things that Chris had said were falling into place, and so many bells were ringing in her head that she was certain at least three dozen angels had suddenly gotten their wings.

She held up a finger to silence him, because he had that look in his eye, as if he was about to ask her why she'd gone all still and crazy on him. But she had to get this out. Because this—*this*—was the pact she'd made with Claire. This was Christmas magic.

This was opportunity knocking hard at her door. "Chris," she said, her voice low and serious. "Are you going to the Starr gala in Santa Fe?"

His eyes widened, and for a moment he looked surprised. Then he nodded. "Yeah."

"Can I go with you?" The words were out of her mouth before she could stop herself. Before she could mentally thwack herself on the head and scream *inappropriate* at the top of her lungs. Especially after her earlier kissing faux pas.

And now all she could do was stare, mortified, and try to process the fact that she'd just invited herself along on a business trip. With a guy she'd just kissed. So that she could try to seduce another guy.

Never mind that Chris was her friend and only her friend.

There were standards. Protocols. What would Emily Post say?

Chris stood up and headed for the kitchen. "You want to leave home and go to Santa Fe while I'm working? Why?"

She stared at the kitchen and listened as he rummaged in her refrigerator. In a minute, he'd return with a diet soda and a string cheese. She'd bet a month's salary on it. "Work," she said. "And bring me one, too. Of both."

He came back with two sodas and two plastic packets of string cheese, and Alyssa mentally patted her intact bank account. "Isn't it the holidays?" he asked.

"Which I'm now spending alone," she said. "At least in Santa Fe I'll have company. You're staying through Christmas, right?" Christmas was in just less than one week, the following Thursday, and she was certain he'd said he'd be back on Saturday.

"You said work," he reminded her. "Why are you working during your holiday break?"

She blew out a mouth full of air and flopped back onto her couch. "I'm getting desperate," she admitted. She hated admitting it, actually, but Chris knew her well enough to know that making partner was more than important to her, it was an absolute requirement.

"And going to Santa Fe ties in how?"

"I want to lock Russell Starr in as a client. I need to bring in a client—and a good one—if I'm going to have any shot at all at partnership."

"And you think you can land him?"

"Yup." No point mentioning that she also wanted a repeat of her late-night kiss with Russell. A kiss that would, hopefully, lead to even more enticing possibilities. "I'm not overwhelmed by the idea of hawking business over the holidays, but the idea of losing partnership isn't exactly doing great things for my stress levels, either."

"But the hotel is booked."

"Right again."

"So I'd be doing you a favor."

"A huge favor," she confirmed, at the same time calling herself six kinds of an idiot. She'd kissed him. And it had felt awesome. The last thing in the world she needed was to be sharing a space with him. It was one thing to remind herself that her across-the-hall neighbor was her best friend and only a friend. It was something completely different to remind herself the same about the guy sleeping in the second double bed.

But if she told him to forget it, she wouldn't get to Santa Fe. And she needed Santa Fe. She needed Russell.

"Chris?"

"It's important to you?"

"Incredibly," she said, sinking deep into the mire.

"Then you're welcome to come. Whatever you need."

"Seriously?"

He took a long swallow of diet soda. "I have a suite and an extra ticket to the gala." He shrugged, his brow furrowed. "We'll have…fun."

Alyssa couldn't believe she'd considered for even a second bowing to Emily Post and the world of good manners. Emily Post could go jump in a lake. This was perfect. *Perfect.*

Except, of course, for part that wasn't perfect at all. Without thinking, she tightened her robe and shoved her hands in her pockets. "Um, you said a suite, right? So that means separate rooms?"

"That's my definition of a suite," he said.

Right. Well. Okay then. That was fine. No impropriety. No awkwardness. Just Alyssa and Chris, and he would still, sort of, be her across-the-hall neighbor. "Okay, then," she said, and then smiled. "Actually, this is going to be great. You're sure, though?" The second the question was out, she regretted it, because what if he took it back? What if he said, "No, just kidding," and claimed he had to work and wasn't allowed a guest. What if there was another girl he'd been hoping to take?

The thought soured in her stomach, the idea of Chris getting all hot and heavy with another woman rubbing her the wrong way. She frowned and tried to erase the image of Chris escorting a stacked, blond bimbette into his hotel room. *So* not going there.

"Alyssa? Hey? Are you listening?"

She wasn't, of course, and realized that she'd heard nothing of what he'd said. "Sorry." She fluttered her fingers by her head. "Holidays, alcohol. My mind's bouncing everywhere. What did you say?"

"I said that I'm sure, and you're welcome to come. I have a pretty limited agenda. The plan is to work, and then work some more."

She thought about his manuscript and outline, now due in just a few days, and the weight of guilt settled back on her shoulders. "Oh, man, I wasn't even thinking. You have to work. I'm going to be a total distraction."

"Nah," he said. "Don't worry about it. You won't distract me. Not at all."

5

SHE WAS GOING TO BE a huge distraction.

Chris tossed another pair of socks into his already overstuffed duffel, and wondered what the hell he'd been thinking last night. The truth was, he hadn't been thinking. Not with his head, anyway. Certain other parts of his anatomy had taken over. The same parts that had sprung to life when Alyssa had kissed him. And those parts had desperately wanted a repeat performance.

And, as always when he thought with his dick instead of his brain, he'd made a bad, bad choice.

Except he didn't regret it. Not one iota.

He was absolutely certain he *would* regret it, when he was sitting in the hotel room, parked in front of his laptop, trying to concentrate while Alyssa moved around, trying to be quiet and not distract him while he worked.

Oh, she'd distract him all right.

Even now, he could remember the way her bare skin had felt against his arm last night. The way she'd stiffened under his touch. The way she'd thrust herself up and closed her mouth over his, hot and demanding and utterly perfect.

She'd been so soft, so vulnerable, and he still couldn't believe that he hadn't hooked his arm under her legs, scooped her up bride-style, and taken her the five feet into her bedroom.

Max Dalton wouldn't have hesitated.

But then again, he wasn't Dalton, which was probably why he wrote the guy, if you wanted to get all pop psychology about it.

And now he'd gone and invited her to stay with him in Santa Fe. Dalton moment if ever there was one. But Dalton wouldn't be playing the we're-just-friends game. Not him. Dalton would be reminding the girl of how nice she'd felt in his arms, and insisting that she discover just how nice naked and between the sheets could be.

Of course, Dalton didn't give a flip about the women in his life come the next morning, or the next night, or the next year, and Chris had absolutely no intention of losing Alyssa. Which meant that the bit of heaven that came with her being near him was also tinged with a bit of hell. Because no matter how much he wanted her—no matter how much he craved her—there wasn't a damn thing he could do about it. Not without risking losing her friendship.

But how was he supposed to look at her—that closely, that intimately—for seven full days and not end up hospitalized for either blue balls or severe insanity? And as for getting any writing done… Well, he was simply going to have to schlep his laptop to the bar and set up shop there. Hemingway wrote with a drink in his hand, didn't he? Maybe that would put some added pizazz in Dalton's adventures.

"Mistake," he muttered to himself as he tried to zip the overstuffed duffel. "The Olympic Gold Medal of mistakes."

"Careful," a deep voice behind him said. "You might start answering yourself."

Chris whipped around. "Dammit, David. I swear I'm going to buy you a cow bell. And what? You're too good to knock on the door?"

"I knocked," Chris's little brother said. "No one answered. Probably because you couldn't hear me over all the chatter in your head. You plotting another book up there?" he asked, tapping his own temple.

"I wish," Chris said darkly.

David's brows lifted as he pulled out the chair by Chris's desk, flipped it around, and straddled it. "Yeah? Who stole the toy out of your Happy Meal?"

"Really not in the mood to talk about it. And I don't have time, either. Airport, remember?" He frowned. "You didn't bring the Mini, did you? Because we're driving Alyssa, too, and—"

"Ah."

That was it. Just a single word. Not even a word, really. Just a breath. But it said it all, and Chris collapsed on the edge of the bed and met his brother's knowing eyes. "A week together in a hotel suite," he said. "I am completely and totally screwed."

David's grin was wicked. "Well, I hope so. You've been hot for the girl for two years now."

Automatically, Chris's eyes darted toward the door, fearing that David had left it open and Alyssa had wandered in. The room was empty, thank God, and he breathed a sigh of relief.

"Interesting," said David. "You're not denying it."

"Gotta face the truth sometime," Chris said. He met his brother's eyes. "I'm a complete shit, aren't I?"

"Absolutely," David agreed amiably. "Why in particular?"

"Because every time I see her I want to rip her clothes off, and I'm letting her stay in my suite without her knowing that. She's probably going to run around in those damn pajama pants and tank tops, and I'm going to spend an entire week being tortured." He ran a hand through his hair. "Actually, maybe she won't. After what happened last night, she'll probably keep her parka on the entire time." He managed a wry grin. "Damn."

"There's a story there," David said. "Spill."

"Just a kiss," Chris said. "But it was some kiss."

David's brow furrowed, and he spun his fingers in the air. "Wait. Back up. You guys had a hot kiss, and yet she's staying in your hotel room wearing her parka? What did I miss?"

"Not what you missed," Chris said. "What *I* missed."

"Okay. What did you miss?"

"The boyfriend train, apparently. I'm a friend and only a friend. Hell, you should have seen the regret painted on her face after she broke from that kiss."

"Who made the first move?"

"Does it matter?"

"Hell yes," David said.

"She did."

"Well, there you go," David said.

"What?"

"The regret," he clarified. "It's bullshit."

"I don't think so," Chris said, although he couldn't deny the tiny spark of hope that was more than willing to jump on the bullshit bandwagon.

"Trust me," his brother said. "Bullshit."

Chris could only wish. He crossed the room, trying to find clean socks. "Bullshit or not, the bottom line is that I'm screwed. I'm supposed to spend the week finishing a book and writing a proposal. Not to mention the article I'm going there for in the first place. How the hell will I be able to focus with Alyssa up close and personal?"

"Telling her might be one way to go. Maybe you'll end up having a Max Dalton-worthy week in bed. Then you can come back inspired and blast out a book proposal."

"No," Chris said, even though that was damn tempting. "She thinks I'm a friend. Even after that kiss, she thinks I'm a safe roommate for the holidays. She has no idea I'm going to be looking at her and wishing I could get her naked."

"Maybe she does," David said. "And maybe that's why she wants to share a room. Hell, maybe that's why she wants to go."

"Don't I wish," Chris said, but he knew damn well it wasn't true. "I'm going to call the resort. Arrange for her to have another room."

"Are there other rooms?"

"I'll work it out," he said, though he didn't have a clue how, because he knew damn well the resort was booked. But he had to do something to get them in separate spaces. Because he wanted her. And having her right there—sharing a suite with him— was too damn close for comfort. Not if he wanted to stay a gentleman. Not if he wanted to keep their friendship intact.

"You're blowing a supreme opportunity, my man," David said as Chris brushed past him for the door, then crossed the hall to Alyssa's apartment. He'd tell her something had come up. He'd tell her to take the suite herself, and he'd take a hotel room in town to write. He could still go to the parties. Could still write his articles. And the up side would be that he would be holed up in an Alyssa-free room, completely distraction-free.

Perfect.

Or not.

He didn't have time to argue with his subconscious, however, because as his knuckles landed on her door in a knock, the door itself pushed open a crack. He started to call for her, but stopped when her voice drifted toward him. He closed his eyes and breathed deep. An entire week in a room with that voice. What kind of an idiot would he be to pass that up?

"Victoria's Secret, Claire!" she was saying with a

laugh. "Trust me. Victoria's about as sexy as my under-wear gets. Not crotchless panties. I mean, come on!"

He considered clearing his throat. Tapping on the door. Something.

He did none of that. Instead, he took a step back-wards and kept on listening. He was only human after all.

"I don't want him to see me as a slut or a one-night stand."

"One-week stand, you mean," Claire corrected, and Chris's stomach tilted awkwardly to the side. Surely they weren't discussing what Alyssa was packing for her week at a hotel with him. Surely David wasn't right and Alyssa had hopes of a Victoria's Secret kind of week with him.

"Right," Alyssa said firmly. "And that's my point. I have one entire week to get him to notice me. To see *me*. Single and female and willing and ready."

Chris swallowed.

"You don't think he's seen you that way before? I mean, that kiss."

Chris's stomach dropped a mile, and his mouth went dry.

"I know. But that was more casual somehow. I'm going for broke here."

Chris wiped sweaty palms on his pants and wondered what the hell he ought to do now. Go in, announce his presence and then call his agent and tell her he'd be spending the week in bed with a woman instead of finishing a manuscript? Or go back quietly to his apartment and let Alyssa's seduction unwind around him?

He had to admit, the seduction concept seemed pretty damned appealing...

He was taking a step backwards when two little words caught his attention.

"Sex toys," Claire said.

"Excuse me?"

"Are you taking some?"

"No!" Alyssa sounded positively appalled. "Are you crazy?"

"No, but apparently I'm a lot more hopeful than you are."

"I don't think he's the sex-toy type," Alyssa said, and Chris cocked his head, thinking that with the right girl he could very much be the type. "And besides, how presumptuous is that? 'Oh, hey! And by the way, lookie what I have in my suitcase?'"

"Sweetie, if this whole trip is about seducing him..."

Chris's brow furrowed. The trip, he'd thought, was about her work.

"The whole trip is about locking up an account," Alyssa countered, her words in perfect accord with his thoughts.

"Uh-huh," said Claire.

"And hopefully getting the guy, too," Alyssa said, and though her tone was almost grudging, he could still hear the smile. Clearly, that had been part of her master plan all along. And a slow grin crept over his face, too. Because that meant *he* had been part of her master plan all along.

Step in, he told himself. *Step in and quit eavesdropping. Do the right thing, dude, and let her know you're here.*

And he was about to—really he was—when Alyssa started talking again. "Do you really think this will work? That he'll notice me? That he'll want me?"

Yes, he wanted to shout.

"I mean, after that drink, he never even called me."

Chris froze, which probably had something to do with the cold chill slowly settling over his body. What drugs had he been on that he would have turned her down?

"You were an idiot to tell Russell about Bob. Of course he wouldn't have called. You were taken. But now," Claire added, "you're not."

Russell.

Chris swallowed as the name banged around in his head like a racquetball. *Not him. Russell.*

She wanted to seduce Russell Starr.

And he was just the idiot who'd gotten her access. Regret curled in his stomach, followed in quick pursuit by the flash burn of anger. No way—*no way*—was he stepping aside and passing Alyssa off to Russell Starr. That was simply not happening, and he closed his hand over the doorknob, ready to push inside and tell her so.

Something, however, stopped him. He was never entirely sure what that something was, but he came to think of it as the spirit of Max Dalton.

And Max was telling him that this wasn't a setback, it was opportunity knocking.

All Chris had to do was open the door.

"YOU WANNA say that again?" David asked. "Because I either heard you wrong, or aliens have taken over my brother's body. What happened to the whole 'She's a friend, she thinks I'm safe' lecture?"

"Let's just say my perspective's changed."

"And now you *want* to seduce Alyssa."

"Hardly a news flash. Are you going to help me or not?" Chris nodded to his solidly closed and locked front door. "She's going to be packed and over here in less than ten minutes, so I need a plan and I need it fast."

David's eyes were narrowed and suspicious, as if he was still waiting for the punch line.

"Dammit, Dave. You did nothing your whole life but seduce girls until Cathy came along and you put a ring on her finger. So give me some help here."

"I still don't get why you need me. You're the one who writes Max Dalton."

"Dalton would pin her to the wall the moment the hotel room door closed behind them."

"What makes you think Alyssa wouldn't like that?"

Chris frowned, then spilled the truth. What he'd overheard. And all about the fact that Alyssa was going on the trip to seduce another man.

"Shit," David said.

"That about sums it up. Got any advice?" Chris still couldn't quite believe that he was asking for help from his former horndog, now happily married brother, but apparently, pigs really did fly.

"Sure. Don't let her see you coming."

Chris shook his head, trying to figure that one out.

"I mean, don't change too abruptly. You guys are friends, right? Play on that. Friends can sit close. Friends can share a glass of wine. Friends can give each other shoulder massages after a sunset hike on a walking trail." He pointed a finger at Chris, a familiar gesture that suggested he was warming to his topic. "She doesn't really want to seduce Russell Starr."

"She sounded pretty serious about the plan," Chris countered.

"Uh-uh," David said, with a firm shake of his head. "She doesn't want to seduce. She wants to *be* seduced. All women do. And right now, for whatever reason, she thinks that Russell can scratch that itch. Your job, my brother, is to prove her wrong."

A sharp knock sounded at the door, and David crossed in that direction, then paused long enough to shoot one firm glance back at Chris. "You've got one hell of an opportunity here, man. Let's see what you can make of it."

Oh, God. Had he really thought he'd be distracted simply from Alyssa being in the suite? He'd been an idiot. That wasn't distraction. That was a mild itch. And now that he knew what she'd planned—not to mention what she'd packed in that suitcase—Chris was flat-out, hands-down, totally screwed.

But as David pulled open the door and Chris saw Alyssa standing there, his heart stuttered in his chest, and he accepted the gauntlet that she wasn't even aware she'd thrown.

The battle between him and Russell Starr was on. And may the best man win.

ALYSSA EYED Chris, currently hunched over under the weight of their combined bags. "Are you sure you don't want me to carry something?"

"I got it," Chris said, though his voice sounded a little strained. No wonder. He'd insisted on hauling his own carry-on bag—a huge backpack with a laptop crammed inside—as well as her computer bag. Which probably wouldn't have been so bad, except that they had landed at one end of the Albuquerque airport, and had about zero-point-seven seconds to get all the way across the airport to their connecting flight.

"You're making me feel like an invalid," Alyssa said. "Not to mention the guilt trip." Truth be told, she was happy to be pampered. As far as Alyssa was concerned, wherever air travel went, pampering should follow.

He stopped, and the smile he shot at her warmed her all the way to her toes. "No guilt," he said firmly. "This saves me a trip to the gym."

"Weight lifting, I hope," she said, "and not racquetball." She nodded to the bag. "That's my computer in there."

"Alyssa."

"Yeah?"

"Go." He nodded down the concourse, and then took off walking. She shook her head, bemused, and followed. She wasn't entirely sure what had come over him, but she knew better than to look a gift packhorse in the mouth.

Not that she had much time to ponder the curiosity. They seriously had to rush to make their connection, and she concentrated on navigating them through the airport at a sprint with Chris getting an aerobic workout beside her.

They were both winded by the time they reached their gate, and Chris let their bags slide to the floor, then collapsed into a hard plastic chair by the windows, breathing hard.

She sank into the chair next to him, holding her sides and laughing. "Never again. I got a workout even without the bags."

"Is this where I say I told you so?"

"Actually, I think it's where I tell you firmly that from now on, every time we travel together, your mantra is 'Alyssa, we need to take the courtesy cart to the opposite end of the airport.'"

His lips twitched. "I'll keep that in mind."

She shook her head. "I'm a sweaty mess."

His eyes met hers, and then his head cocked sideways, as if he was seriously weighing her words. "Nah. You look great."

In her chest, her heart did a little skittering number and her breath hitched. "If you say I glow, I'll have to smack you," she retorted, trying to bring the moment back to center. Back to the place where she wasn't looking at her best guy friend *that* way.

Not that she got to spend a lot of time worrying,

because a flight attendant at the door started waving wildly at them. "Flight 207? Come on, come on! The last shuttle's about to leave!"

Alyssa looked at Chris, who looked right back at her: *shuttle?*

"THERE ARE propellers," she said, leaning close to Chris and raising her voice so as to be heard over the roar of said props. "Pro-pel-lers," she repeated, emphasizing each syllable, in case he'd missed the import of this terrible, horrible fact of life. "Are those even legal anymore?"

She'd known it was going to be bad when they'd been herded onto a bus and taken across the tarmac to a plane that had to have been in the air during the Second World War. Honestly, she should have run in the opposite direction the moment the girl at the gate had said the S-word. *Shuttle.*

Chris leaned closer still, so close that the scent of his cologne mixed with sweat seemed to fill the space between them. It was a masculine scent, and she leaned in, telling herself it wasn't about the way he smelled, but about trying to hear him over the roar of the engines. Unfortunately, she didn't quite believe herself.

"It's perfectly safe," he said, closing his hand over hers. "You trust me, right?"

She closed her hand so that her fingers were clutching the armrest between them, and clutching it tightly. Because otherwise she might turn her hand over and close hers around his. "I trust you, sure. But I don't know the pilot. What if he's incompetent? Or worse, overly arrogant. What if he thinks he can handle it, but he can't? What if we fall from the sky?"

He frowned, as if seriously considering the point. "We won't. I'm pretty sure the laws of physics are on our side."

"And the law of gravity?" she asked. "Whose side is it on? Huh?"

"You're right," he said, looking shocked. "We'd better assume crash positions." He leaned forward, his head to his knees, leaving her upright and giggling.

"Okay, okay. Maybe I'm being a little bit melodramatic, but it's really—I don't know. Creeping me out." She'd never been in a prop plane before, and the decibel level combined with the vibration was not giving her a warm fuzzy feeling.

Chris's eyes narrowed as he looked at her. "You're really scared."

"Hello? Yes."

"It'll be fine," he said seriously. "You know I wouldn't lie to you."

She swallowed, then nodded, because she did know that. Chris was—well, he was Chris. And if he said that they would survive the death trap, then survive it they would.

"Do you usually fly in these things?" she asked. "When you do your articles?"

"Not much," he said. "I fly first class more than I fly prop, and believe me when I say that the magazine rarely pays for first class."

"But you have?"

"Sure. Once in Mexico. Landed in the dirt. Thought it was an emergency landing, actually, but it turns out that's where the plane always touches down. And once in Africa. Safari trip."

"Well, that's something," she said, envious of all his travel despite the prop planes. "I mean, you're still alive, right?"

"Last time I checked."

"Okay," she said, tugging her hand free and holding them both tight in her lap. "But if we crash and die, I'm never speaking to you again."

"That's probably fair," he said. He shifted, pulling his hand away so that he could reach for the laptop he'd stowed under the seat. It was a perfectly normal move, and a perfectly normal thing to do on a plane. But even so, the moment he shifted away from her, she was struck by an unwelcome sense of loss coupled with the urge to reach out and grab his hand again. Only to keep herself calm, because of the plane-falling-out-of-the-sky issue. That's all.

But she couldn't do it. Not casually. Not without it seeming like she wanted to, you know, *hold hands*.

And she didn't. She just wanted moral support. Emotional support. A soft cushion if the plane descended to the ground in a massive ball of fire.

Because right then, without his hand, she felt incredibly unprotected.

Ironic, she supposed, since this was Chris she was talking about. *Chris.* Her friend. And no matter how soothing he might be, no matter how calm and steadfast he stood in a storm or a vibrating prop plane, Christopher Hyde was *not* her Knight in Shining Armor. He wasn't the guy who could sweep her off her feet and keep her safe and secure for ever after.

He was her friend, pure and simple. And no matter how many errant thoughts slipped into her head, he was staying that way.

With a sigh she leaned her head back against the worn upholstery and tried to ignore the billion-decibel hum of the propellers. Russell probably had a private jet. Not a single prop in sight. And with that thought, she closed her eyes and imagined she was in that jet, with private flight attendants bringing them drinks, and Russell beside her, telling her that he didn't know how he'd lived without her all these years. That he wanted to give his business to her firm, and his heart to her.

Visualization, right? That's what all the self-help books said. Visualize your goal and then go for it.

She saw him then, walking toward her in that imaginary jet, his body tall and lean, his hands strong and smooth. She couldn't quite picture his face, but that didn't matter. She knew who he was; she knew what she wanted.

And she was going full-tilt toward her goal.

6

BESIDE DALTON, Natalia slept, her head tilted toward the plane's window, her lips parted in sweet surrender.

He pressed his own lips together, wanting to know the taste of her. Wanting to feel her soft flesh under his mouth. Despite his initial qualms, she'd handled herself brilliantly on their mission.

Now he wanted nothing more than to handle her.

His fingers twitched with the desire to stroke smooth skin. To watch the pulse in her throat quicken. To see her face flush with desire.

They'd come together on this mission to capture the enemy.

He'd never once expected that she'd capture his heart. Him. Max Dalton. A man who tied himself to no single woman.

Not until now, anyway.

At the front of the plane, a door opened, and a woman stepped in. Long and lean, she wore a tailored outfit with a jaunty blue cap perched on perfectly coiffed hair. The pair of gold wings pinned above her breast twinkled in the dim light of the cabin. She paused in *front of the few other passengers, bending down to take drink orders and inquire as to her charges' comfort. Her eyes, however, never left Max. Finally, she made her way to his side.*

"Mr. Dalton," she said, her voice husky. "Is there anything you need?" She bent to pick up the empty cup from his tray table, and her blouse gaped open, revealing perfect breasts barely hidden behind stark white lace. "Coffee? Tea?" Her glossy mouth curved knowingly. "Anything at all."

He waited for the familiar tightening in his crotch, a sexual frustration he knew well how to satisfy, only to be even more frustrated that the keening need didn't arise. He wanted nothing from this woman, and that reality settled around him like a new jacket, unfamiliar and yet distinctly comfortable. "Nothing," he said, firmly meeting her gaze. "Nothing at all."

One brow quirked upward. "You're sure?"

"I am."

She pulled a gun from her pocket. "That's unfortunate, Mr. Dalton. Because I don't handle rejection well. Not well at all."

CHRIS SCOWLED at his computer screen. *Problem.* Yup. This was definitely going to be a problem.

He shifted in his seat so that he could look at his problem, still asleep next to him.

Damn.

What the hell had he been thinking? Less than two weeks to finish the book and outline the next, and he couldn't even think straight because of the woman beside him.

He felt his ears pop and realized they were starting their descent. Beside him, Alyssa's lips were moist and parted in sleep, just like Natalia's on his pages. His own mouth went dry, his body hard, as he remembered the way those lips had felt against his. How he wished they would feel again.

The way she would sound, a low moan rising in her throat, even as her hands clutched his head, fingers clutching tighter, pulling closer, deepening the kiss to such an intensity he could almost come just thinking about it.

He opened his eyes and realized he was hard as a rock, and damn happy he had both a blanket and a computer on his lap to cover all evidence of his train of thought.

Beside him, Alyssa's eyes remained closed, her breathing soft. Lust hadn't interrupted her sleep, and arousal wasn't coloring her dreams. Any illusions he had that she'd felt a spark of desire when she'd looked at him probably fell more accurately into the realm of *de*lusion.

She wants to be seduced, David's voice reminded him. The trouble, of course, was that she wanted to be seduced by a man other than Chris. Which made Chris's fantasies that she'd somehow end up in his bed this week seem utterly impossible

Except he had to try, right? He might not want to lose Alyssa's friendship, but even more, he didn't want to lose her to another man. The big green beast of jealousy had raised its head, and Chris was in the game.

.Trouble was, he wasn't entirely familiar with the rules of engagement.

Because while Chris might be able to write about a guy who said all the right things to women and eased them comfortably between the sheets, real life was a different story.

"I THINK we're lost." Alyssa squinted at the map of Santa Fe that had come with the rental car and idly wondered if it would make more sense if she read it upside down. "See? That building right there. We've passed it twice already."

"Are we still on St. Francis Drive?" Chris asked.

"Um…" She swiveled in her seat. "Paseo de Peralta," she said, catching a glimpse of a passing sign. "How did we get on this street?"

"I'm guessing a wrong turn," he said, then shot her a sideways look. "Either that, or evil fairies."

"My navigational skills are above reproach," she said, turning the map back so that north once again faced up. "I think your fairy hypothesis has merit."

"Okay, navigator. Which way do I need to go to get back where we need to be?"

"Are you asking me a literal question, or are we talking from an overall philosophical perspective?"

"Let's stick with your basic left, right, north, south."

She rolled her eyes in mock exasperation. "You're just no fun at all." Which was *so* not true. She'd laughed more getting to this point than she had in ages.

"I'm turning here," he said, making a left onto Palace. "Now what?"

"Well, hang on. Now I have to figure out where—"

"Ha!" he said, pointing out his window. "Downtown Santa Fe." He looked smugly in her direction. "And I'm not even the one with the map."

"I offered to drive, but you insisted I navigate. If we end up completely lost, I figure that makes you half-responsible."

"I can live with that."

"And why do we care about downtown? The resort's on the outskirts."

"Because I'm starving. Let's eat now, then find the resort. Otherwise, I may eat the sugarplums and peppermint sticks that will undoubtedly be decorating the lobby, and that never goes over well with hotel staff. Besides," he added, "I want to take in some of the local color."

"Well, you certainly have it here," she said, looking around at the famous Plaza area. The sun had set about fifteen minutes earlier, and now electric lights twinkled on the stores that surrounded the famous park and landmark war memorial. *Farolitos*—candles in brown paper bags—lined the sidewalks, illuminating the blanket of snow that covered the grass and gave the area an even more magical feel. "Park here," she said. "There's got to be someplace fabulous to eat nearby."

As he pulled in, she saw a dog bounding forward, unhindered by either the dragging leash or by the antlers affixed to his head and lit up with tiny Christmas lights.

"They get into the spirit of the season here," Chris said dryly.

"I love it." She opened her door, and the piquant scent of burning piñon wood wafted over her. "Oh, my God," she said, breathing deeply. "Can I just stay here for the rest of the trip and breathe?"

"I think you'd require some food eventually. Speaking of which—" He nodded across the plaza to a street lined with adobe storefronts. "Right there. Looks like a restaurant."

They walked that way, and sure enough they found themselves outside of a restaurant called Jorge's with an outside bar, complete with wood-burning outdoor fireplaces to keep guests cozy while they waited for a table. And, yeah, they had to wait. At first, Alyssa had almost demurred, insisting that they go on to the resort and eat something at the hotel.

But she'd kept her mouth shut. Despite the cold, there was something enchanting in the way the night had settled over the town, and with the lights twinkling and the wood burning, she had absolutely no desire to leave. Not right then. Not when she was having such a great time with Chris.

It was, she thought, the perfect way to unwind before she went to work. Dinner in a fabulous restaurant with a good friend. Because once she got to the resort, she *would* be working. Working to get the client, and working to get the man.

In front of her, Chris was speaking with the hostess, and she eyed his back, admiring the way his broad shoulders filled out the coat he wore. The night was un-seasonally warm for Santa Fe, but still they were bundled up, not at all like the locals who were taking advantage of the "warm spell" and running around in light coats instead of the down-filled parkas she and Chris wore.

He turned, his smile aimed only at her, then gestured her forward. He took her elbow casually, then started to steer her into the outdoor bar area. "About thirty minutes for a table, but I said that was okay. I hope you don't mind. I thought we could wait over here by the fire until they called us."

Thirty minutes for a table, then an hour or so to eat. Time was ticking away, and once again, she was struck by the realization that if she had any hope of finding Russell this evening, she really should get moving. Except she didn't want to get going. Maybe it was because as soon as she got to the hotel the reality of her missions would be inescapable. The pressure would be on, and she'd lose out on the quiet pleasure of hanging out with Chris, lifting a glass of wine and laughing as though she didn't have a care in the world.

She realized with a start that Chris was staring at her. She shifted, feeling almost naked under the force of his gaze. "What?" She brushed her lips, wondering if her makeup was smeared.

"The firelight," he said, tilting his head to indicate the firepit beside their table, but not taking his eyes off her. "It makes your eyes sparkle."

"Oh." She blushed, pleased by the compliment,

then focused her attention on the wine menu. "So, um, do you want to get a couple of glasses? Or should we open a bottle?"

"A bottle," he said, then smiled when she looked up at him. "Let's live dangerously."

There was nothing unusual about his tone, or even about his words. But even so, she found herself swallowing, the echo of that word—*dangerously*—ringing in her mind.

She sat up straighter and tried to get her head back where it belonged. "I'm all for danger," she said, with the kind of smile she'd always reserved for Chris. A best friend, let's-hang-out kinda smile. The kind of smile she needed to conjure before she embarrassed herself again with the guy who was giving her a free place to crash for a week.

Oh, Lord.

Clearly she'd made a huge mistake. No way should she be sharing a room with Chris. Maybe she'd crossed into another dimension when she'd kissed him yesterday, but he was seriously messing with her head lately—and her thoughts were straying far too frequently away from best-friend parameters.

And those kinds of thoughts were unacceptable. She repeated the word in her head, just to make sure she got it: *Un.Ac.Cept.A.Ble.*

"I have a confession to make," he said, after he'd put in their order for a bottle of Shiraz. "I had an ulterior motive for not wanting to go straight to the resort."

"Oh." She swallowed, and despite the little pep talk

she'd just had with herself, the word *ulterior* conjured decadent—and inappropriate—images. *Dang it.* She needed to stop acting like a spazz. "A little last-minute Christmas shopping at some of the local galleries? A secret desire to stand on a street corner and sing Christmas carols?"

"Both undeniably appealing," he said. "But no. I thought I'd do some Max Dalton research, and I was hoping you'd help me out."

"Yeah? That sounds like fun. What do I have to do?"

"Just be yourself," he said, but something in the way he said it made her tingle all over. She was determined to stay calm, cool and centered. And in a non-sexual, all-friend frame of mind. "How is me being me going to help you?"

"Part of the next book is set here," he said. "I want to look around. Go into places Dalton would go into. Step into his shoes for a while."

"I thought the Dalton books were all international."

"It's just a couple of scenes," he said. "I want to take advantage of being on location. I need to do a blog entry tonight anyway for the magazine. I figure why not research for the blog and for Dalton." He paused, and the silence hung between them, full of anticipation. "Are you game?"

"Sure. Sounds like fun."

"That's all I wanted to hear."

The waiter returned with a bottle of wine at the same time the hostess announced their table was ready. Alyssa almost didn't want to leave the magic of the outdoor bar for the bustle of the dining room, but her stomach had other ideas, and once they were inside and the delicious scent of Southwestern cooking wafted over them, she seriously considered simply curling up right there in the booth and moving in forever.

"I HAVE DIED and gone to heaven," she said as she pushed her plate away, too stuffed to eat another bite. "That posole was amazing," she added, referring to the traditional pork and hominy stew the waiter had recommended.

"Does that mean you don't want to try a bite of mine?" Chris asked, holding up a forkful of chicken in a chile lime sauce that smelled divine.

"You're cruel, you know that? Very cruel."

He moved the fork closer across the table. "It's delicious. Come on, Alyssa. Quit fighting it. You know you want to."

She squirmed, his words filling her. Teasing her. "I—"

"No more excuses," he said, then leaned forward, leading with the fork. She opened her mouth, then closed it around the warm tines of his fork. Chris's fork. The same fork that had been in his mouth moments before.

She closed her eyes and pulled back, concentrating on the food, the food and nothing but the food.

Which wasn't hard, as it was hands-down the most delicious bite of chicken she'd ever tasted.

She opened her eyes, planning to tell him so, and saw that his eyes were already on her. On her mouth, actually. And when his gaze moved slowly over her face to her eyes, for the briefest of moments, Alyssa saw desire hidden in those golden-brown depths.

She pulled away and concentrated on swallowing, one finger reaching to curl a strand of hair around itself. Her own lust-filled thoughts she could handle. But they couldn't go there together. Both of them getting ideas…well, that was a bad thing. Friends and sex didn't mesh. And the thought of losing Chris the way she'd lost Bob…well, she couldn't even wrap her head around it.

"You have a little—"

"What?" she asked, as he leaned forward, his napkin in his hand.

"Cheese," he said, but he didn't brush it away with his napkin. Instead, he dragged his thumb just beneath her lower lip, the caress so gentle it had Alyssa stifling a small gasp of pleasure. "There," he said, pulling his thumb away. "That's better."

The sudden lack of contact distressed her, leaving her aware of a chill on her skin where his thumb had caressed her. *No,* she thought. *Not better. Not better at all.*

She blinked and stood, grabbing her purse. "I—I have to hit the ladies' room. Meet me on the sidewalk?"

"Sure," he said, but she was already gone.

As she walked away, she could feel his eyes on her back, watching her, and so she didn't relax until she'd turned the corner by the restrooms. Then she sagged against the wall, closed her eyes and wondered what in hell she'd gotten herself into.

CHRIS SLAMMED back the rest of his wine, closed his eyes and then swallowed the rest of Alyssa's wine, as well. He wasn't at all nervous about being with Alyssa—after all, this was Alyssa he was talking about—but he was nervous as hell about where it might be leading.

Because, although he'd been following David's advice and acting around her the way he always did, today there'd been one subtle change: He hadn't held back.

Before, he'd always watched himself. Always made certain not to cross lines. To keep their friendship at the forefront and downplay the fact that he was a guy and she was a girl, and there was some serious chemistry working between the two of them.

But now that he knew she wanted sparks popping between her and another guy, downplaying wasn't on the agenda. He wanted to see the kind of heat in her eyes he'd seen that night in her apartment. Heat, lust, desperate take-me-now kind of passion, that was goal number one.

And damned if he didn't see it spark between them just now.

Russell Starr, you are going down.

He eyed the bottle of wine, wondering if he should drink down the last little bit, just to keep up his courage, then decided against it. A little buzz was one thing. Too much, though, and he might start belting out love songs as they strolled the shops that lined the famous plaza. Not exactly subtle.

Best to skip the last bit of wine.

He met up with her on the sidewalk in front of the restaurant. Her face was bright, most of her makeup gone, and the hair around her face was damp. "You okay?"

"Just splashed some water on my face," she said. "We've been up since the crack of dawn, and I'm starting to fade. I, um, realized I've been acting a little loopy. Zoning out. That kind of thing." Her mouth curled up in a half smile. "Sorry."

"Nothing to worry about," he said. "I hadn't noticed the slightest bit of loopiness. To me, you're just Alyssa, and loopy or not, I'm glad you came with me."

It was difficult to tell in the dim light, but he thought she flushed. And he was certain that her smile was filled with pleasure. For a moment—one brief, fleeting moment—guilt curled in his stomach. Because he'd changed the rules without telling her. He'd shifted the dynamic between them, and he was playing for keeps.

She, however, wasn't playing at all.

"Are *you* okay?" Now it was Alyssa's turn to stare at him.

"I'm great," he said. "Guess I'm a little tired, too." Then, in case she had any ideas about cutting the evening short, he extended his arm and waited for her to take it. "I have Dalton coming here to intercept a message," he said, which despite the fact that he'd made that tidbit up on the fly, didn't sound like such a bad idea. "I want to figure out the best location."

He glanced sideways at her as they walked, noticing the way she pursed her lips as she thought. "Probably something that's a Santa Fe staple, right? Not necessarily a Christmas thing."

"Exactly," he said.

"Claire said that there's a Native American arts program, and locals sell jewelry at the, um, Governor's Palace. Or maybe it's the—"

"Palace of the Governors," he said. "I read that, too, and it didn't even occur to me what a great pass location that would make for a spy. You're brilliant," he said, meaning it.

"Thanks. I aim to please." She frowned, then peered around the Plaza. "But where is this place? And will there still be people out after dark?"

"It's not even seven yet," he reminded her, the dark coming earlier in the mountains than in Dallas. "Plus it's the holidays, and there are tourists aplenty. I bet they're still out. If I were selling something, I know I would be."

"Fair enough. Now all we have to do is find the place."

That turned out to be an easy enough task, and soon they were walking along the portal of the Palace of the Governors, smiling at the vendors, many of whom seemed as old as the mountains surrounding them.

"Look at this," Alyssa said, pulling him to the side and showing him an ornate, diamond-shaped creation woven from colored cotton yarn, feathers, beads and bits of leather.

"What is it?"

"A dream catcher," she said. "Claire would love it, don't you think?"

Chris thought of Alyssa's friend and had to concede that impulsive Claire would probably be thrilled with a present like that.

"We bumped Christmas to next Monday," Alyssa said. "Since you and I are here on the actual day, she'll come over to my place then and we're going all out with turkey and fixings." She looked back over her shoulder as she paid the artist. "Will you still come, too?"

Chris didn't even need a moment to think. "I'll bring the mashed potatoes. I can boil and mash like a pro."

"Great." She laughed and took his arm, a shopping bag now swinging from her other hand as they walked, eyeing the wares, most of which consisted of amazing silver jewelry.

"My mom," Chris said, eyeing a pair of earrings. "Surely the hotel has shipping, don't you think?"

"Sure," Alyssa said. "And she'll love them. Your dad?"

"I could get him a giant cow belt buckle," Chris said, nodding to one displayed on the ground. "But I already got him a subscription to *Farm & Ranch* and a gift card for Home Depot. The man's really not hard to shop for."

"Guess not. Are you bummed not to be going home this year?"

He looked at her, then shook his head. "I miss them, of course, but I'm perfectly content with my current holiday scenario."

"Oh," she said, her eyes cutting down to skim the vendors' wares. "Yeah. Me, too."

"Now, this is nice," Chris said, after they'd walked down a few more slots. He had paused in front of a large, gray blanket covered with leather bracelets ornamented with etched silver. An elderly man sat cross-legged on the blanket, a thin pipe in his mouth, piercing blue eyes almost hidden by the craggy folds of his leathery face. His hair was white-gray, and he had an air of mystery.

If Chris had any doubts about including this as a scene in the next Dalton book, those doubts dissolved in a puff. This was perfect. He eyed Alyssa out of the corner of his eye, saw that she'd bent down to look more closely at the bracelets.

Yeah, he thought, absolutely perfect.

"The craftsmanship is amazing," he said, picking up a delicate bracelet in which the silver band that covered the leather was etched with designs so intricate Chris could only assume they were both ancient and held deep meaning.

The old man bent his head. "I thank you for your kindness." He turned his head to look at Alyssa, then shifted his attention back to Chris. "You wish perhaps to buy something for your woman?"

"I—"

"Oh," Alyssa said, taking a step backwards and shaking her head. "He's, um, not my boyfriend."

Chris couldn't decide if he should be frustrated that she was so quick to deny, or pleased that the vendor was so quick to assume. He decided to go with pleased— better to think positively. And maybe the old man had picked up on a vibe.

"We're friends," he said, reaching over to take Alyssa's hand. "Good friends."

The old man's eyes, already nearly invisible behind the peaks and valleys of his face, seemed to narrow as he looked at Chris. *Looked,* Chris thought, *and saw.*

Chris cleared his throat, not uncomfortable so much as fearful that Alyssa would look at the old man's face and see reflected there the truth in Chris's heart. A truth he was concealing. At least for now.

"This, then," the old man said, reaching to the far side of the blanket and lifting a bracelet. Like the one Chris had earlier been inspecting, this, too, was intricately made, the craftsmanship apparent. "For friendship," he said. He looked once again to Chris and pressed a hand over his heart. "A true friend resides here forever."

"That's nice," Alyssa said.

"I'll take it," Chris said. He turned to Alyssa. "Will you let me buy it for you?"

"Chris, you can't."

"Sure I can," he said. "I just reach into my pocket and pull out my wallet." He demonstrated while she rolled her eyes in mock exasperation.

"Excuse us," she said to the artist, pulling Chris a few feet away. "You don't need to be buying me things," she said. "You have more important things to worry about. Like rent. And food."

"I'm not destitute," Chris said, regretting that very first conversation in which he'd admitted to her that he was behind on his rent because he'd turned down an assignment in order to keep two solid weeks free for polishing his first manuscript. And while he liked the fact that she cared enough to worry about him, she obviously feared he was going to be in line at a soup kitchen any day now.

"Fine," she said tartly. "You're not destitute. But you've already bought me a Christmas present."

"True," he agreed, having more fun than he should trying to convince her to let him buy the bracelet. "But this one's not for any particular occasion."

"I don't know…"

"One bracelet isn't going to break me," he said. "And we're friends, aren't we?"

She drew in a breath, then nodded. "The best," she said, and it was probably only wishful thinking that he heard a bit of heat in her voice.

"Let's try it on," he said, edging back toward the blanket the artisan had spread out on the sidewalk. He shot her a grin. "After all, Dalton could get the information passed to him etched on a piece of jewelry."

Her lip twitched as she held out her arm. "So this is all book research?"

"Maybe not all," he confessed, letting his thumb graze the soft skin on the back of her wrist before he fastened the clasp.

She swallowed audibly. Her green eyes seemed to sparkle in the dim light, and she drew her arm away slowly, then held her wrist up to look at the bracelet, her own thumb brushing gently over the place where he'd touched her. On purpose? Or a reflex. He didn't know—didn't want to read anything more into the moment than what was really there.

Hell, he didn't want to get his hopes up.

But he couldn't help it. He was aware of his own heartbeat, his own breathing.

And he was damn sure aware of the woman standing next to him.

Bottom line? Yeah, he was cautiously optimistic.

So sue him.

He turned his attention back to the vendor. "How much do I owe you?"

The price quoted was more than reasonable, especially as Chris would have easily paid quadruple that simply for the pleasure of seeing Alyssa wearing a gift from him.

They said goodbye and moved on down the row to peruse the other crafts and wares displayed for purchase. Chris, however, paid attention to none of it. Instead, his head was spinning. He'd scored serious points tonight. Of that, he was absolutely certain.

"Chris, look."

Her hand closed over his elbow, and the casual intimacy of the gesture about brought him to his knees. She was sweet torture, and she didn't even realize it.

He pasted on a smile and tried to look casual. "What?"

"There's a fireplace on the sidewalk."

Sure enough, a local restaurant had a firepit located at the edge of their outdoor seating area, providing warmth to passersby and luring the crowds in close with a promise of warmth and a drink. The scent of burning piñon wood filled the air, and the pull was inescapable. "You up for another drink?"

For a moment, he feared she'd hesitate, claiming she wanted to get to the resort. But to his delight, she smiled and nodded, then even took his hand, her fingers lacing through his. "Come on," she said, her grin playful. "Maybe if we ask nice they'll let us toast marshmallows."

The hostess seated them one table away from the fire, and the heat seemed to waft over them, warm and delicious. Soothing and relaxing. Relaxed, he thought, was good. Relaxed, and she just might let down her guard.

They decided on warm mulled wine served in stoneware goblets, and after it was poured, he lifted his in a toast. "To a perfect beginning."

"It has been, hasn't it?" she said as she tapped her goblet against his. "Thanks for letting me tag along. We haven't even arrived, and I'm having a great time."

"No thanks necessary," he said. He kept his eyes on hers, but reached over to gently brush the bracelet she now wore. The one that in his mind marked her as belonging to him. "That's what friends are for, right?"

She swallowed, then looked down as she raised the goblet to her lips. Honestly, she looked rattled. Good. He wanted her rattled. Wanted her confused. Wanted her to forget her mission to seduce Russell and fall into his own arms instead. His arms and his life.

"A rose for the lady?"

Chris looked up, surprised to see the small woman who'd stepped up, holding a wicker basket full of fragrant roses.

"I—sure," he said, thrilled to see delight light in Alyssa's eyes as he paid for the flower.

"I can't remember the last time someone bought me a rose," she said. "That's sweet."

"You're welcome," he said, passing her the perfect red flower.

She closed her eyes and bent to smell it, and he imagined that when she looked up again, he'd see the fire of desire in her eyes. She'd smile at him. Those lips would part, and she'd say his name, ever so softly—

"Russell."

Chris blinked. *Not* what he'd expected. "What?"

"Sorry," she said, looking over his shoulder. "But that's Russell Starr."

Chris bit back a curse and turned in his seat. Russell was striding right toward them, a smile stretched wide on that pretty-boy face, his arms wide in greeting.

Chris might be reality, but from the spark that flashed in Alyssa's eyes, there was no denying that Russell was pure fantasy.

And how the hell did Chris compete with that?

7

"ALYSSA CHAMBERS." Russell crossed the seating area, his hands outstretched, his expression one of such pleasure that Alyssa couldn't help but smile in return even though, dammit, she was completely rattled.

No. No rattling allowed. This was *Russell,* the man she'd come to New Mexico to see. It wasn't as if he was interrupting a date—there were no date vibes going on between her and Chris. None whatsoever.

Or, if there were, then the interruption was probably a good thing, because there sure as hell shouldn't be date vibes.

Friend vibes, yes. Date vibes, no.

Dear God, she was rambling in her own head.

Rattled. She was *so* definitely rattled.

She tamped it down and stood up, forcing her manners to work even if her head wasn't functioning properly. "Russell, it's great to see you."

He took her hand, then leaned forward for a quick kiss on the cheek. She waited for that spark of heat as his lips grazed her skin. For the urge to turn her lips toward his. She waited for her pulse to dance and her breath to hitch.

They didn't.

Instead, she simply stood there, slightly embarrassed and feeling completely awkward that her first meeting with Russell was in the presence of Chris.

Which, when she thought about it, made perfect sense. After all, she wanted to leave Santa Fe with both the job and the guy, and yet she'd only mentioned the job part of the equation to Chris. So of course she'd feel uncomfortable around Russell if Chris was present.

And that, Alyssa, is a load of crap.

The truth was that she felt weird because she was now in close proximity to two men she found desperately attractive. But she intended to pursue only one of them.

Awkward much?

Very.

Russell pulled back from her, but his hand lingered on her elbow as he turned and looked at Chris, who'd stood, his eyes gone hard and wary. "Russell Starr," he said. "And you're Alyssa's date?"

"No," Alyssa said before Chris could answer. "He's my friend. A really good friend, but just a friend." She smiled at Chris, and although she was only relaying the God's honest truth, she felt like an absolute heel for saying the words out loud. Because claiming Chris as a friend meant denying everything else.

And somehow, despite the fact that she'd long ago made the decision to do that very thing, that denial sat heavy in her stomach.

"Christopher Hyde," Chris said, holding out his hand. "We're on our way to your resort, actually."

"Hyde," Russell repeated. "You're the reporter *Tourist and Travel* is sending."

"That would be me." Chris's mouth quirked in a quick smile. "Alyssa's my roommate for the weekend."

"Is she?" Russell asked, looking between the two of them.

"We're just friends," Alyssa said quickly. "The hotel was completely booked. And since Chris has a suite, he offered to let me bunk with him."

"I can probably help with that," Russell said, his eyes solely on her. "Give me a buzz tomorrow and we'll see if we can't find you a room of your own."

"Oh." Alyssa managed a smile, uncomfortable with how bitter the thought of leaving Chris tasted. "Sure. I can do that."

"Actually," Russell said, raising his hand to signal to someone behind them, "why don't you two come horseback-riding tomorrow morning? Say eleven-thirty?" He turned to Chris as a reedy blonde in a painted-on dress sidled over. "I imagine you'd like an interview for your article, and we could do it on the trail."

"Thanks," Chris said, looking genuinely pleased. "We'll do that."

Alyssa blinked. Not only did she and horses not get along, but the idea of spending her first day at the resort with both Chris and Russell was decidedly surreal.

Then again, if the blonde who'd hooked her arm through Russell's was any indication, she didn't have a chance with him anyway.

"Alyssa, Chris, this is Mandy Petrie, my dinner date."

"A pleasure," Mandy said, with a smile that must have made some dentist a very rich man.

Russell turned to go. "So tomorrow, then? The lobby. Eleven-thirty?"

Alyssa met Chris's eyes, hoping hers didn't reflect how completely bamboozled she felt. He nodded, and she turned her head up to look at Russell. "Great. We can't wait."

She sank back into her seat as they walked away, closing her eyes until she'd pulled herself together enough to look at Chris again.

"Well," he said, his expression unreadable. "Tomorrow should be interesting."

And that, thought Alyssa, probably qualified for the understatement of the year.

THE LOBBY of the Santa Fe Starr bustled, and Chris and Alyssa had to squeeze past groups of holiday revelers in order to get to the counter to check in. Not that Chris minded. The crush of people simply meant that Alyssa was forced to stand closer to him, as there wasn't enough floor space to go around.

He welcomed the proximity, especially after their encounter with Russell at the bar. Since then, Alyssa had been quieter, more withdrawn, and the casual flirting that had zinged in the air between them had died a quick, painful death.

Chris told himself he wasn't worried. After all,

Russell had been escorting another woman, who really didn't look to be the type who shared. Then again, Russell had taken care to introduce her as his *dinner* date. Not his date. Not his girlfriend. Not his cousin from Connecticut.

His dinner date.

As in subtly telling Alyssa that he was available for all other dating times and functions.

Bastard.

His turn at the counter forced a quick end to his mental burning of Russell in effigy. Soon he had the key to his deluxe junior suite, along with his Holiday Activities Guide, and he and Alyssa were following an efficient bellman down a covered path to a row of bungalows. The smell of woodburning fireplaces filled the air, and Chris breathed deep, thinking that this was the kind of place you brought a girl on a honeymoon. Not where you brought a girl who thought she'd rather be with another guy.

"Busy back there," he said to Alyssa, and then kicked himself. They'd been friends for two years, and he sounded like Office Drone A making small talk with Executive Z.

"I think today's the day most people are checking in. I bet it's calmer tomorrow."

"Oh, yeah," the bellman said. "We've been scrambling today to get everyone to their proper rooms, but everything should even out tomorrow." He pointed down the path. "You're on the left, just past the first set of stairs. I'm going to take the long way around since

I need a ramp for the cart." He veered off, leaving Chris and Alyssa standing together in what felt, for the first time since he'd known her, like an awkward silence.

She cleared her throat. "I hope he's right about the craziness calming down. I still need to schedule a meeting with Russell, and I think that may be harder than I anticipated."

"I'm sure it won't be a problem," he said dryly.

She looked sideways at him as they ascended the small set of stairs. "What's with you?"

"Nothing." He shrugged, because the truth was that it was everything. She wanted Russell. Had come on this trip specifically for the purpose of catching Russell. And from what Chris could see, Russell was going to be more than happy to be caught.

"Whatever it is, it's not nothing," she said.

"Forget it," he said, then drew in a breath and forced himself to center. "I'm certain Russell will give you a meeting."

"Great," she said, then narrowed her eyes at him. "Why do I get the feeling that *you* don't think that's great?"

Maybe because he wanted Alyssa to want *him*, not Russell, and the abrupt change in her demeanor after Russell had appeared had both frustrated and saddened him. How the hell was he supposed to compete with the likes of Russell Starr? A man who had wit and charm and millions in the bank?

Not that he could tell her any of that.

"Chris?" she prodded.

"Nothing," he said. "I'm just tired."

"Oh." But she kept curious eyes on him.

They'd reached the door, and he slid his card key through the lock, then held the door open for her. She squeezed past him, and when they were even with each other in the doorway, he met her eyes. "It's just that I—"

"What?" she asked, sounding exasperated.

"I want you to be careful," he said, spitting the words out. "With Starr, I mean. I'd hate to see you end up having a fling with some guy who's only about the moment."

He held his breath, waiting for the inevitable denial. Waiting for her to reassure him it was only about business.

The reassurance didn't come.

Instead, her teeth dragged along her lower lip, and she looked everywhere but at his face. "I can handle myself."

"So you're not interested?" he asked hopefully, because he desperately needed her to deny any and all interest in Russell Starr other than as a means to saving her job.

She didn't answer. Just shifted her attention to the room that opened out in front of them. She took a step in and he followed, almost walking into her back when she stopped short.

"Alyssa?"

She turned, the expression on her face a combination of confusion and horror. "Um, Chris? Where's the other bedroom?"

OBJECTIVELY, the room was stunning. Alyssa took it all in, marveling at the thoughtful decorating that combined Native American– and Southwest-style art and architecture with undeniably modern amenities. A woven rug covered the wooden floor as they walked in, and to the right a small kitchenette greeted them. Beyond that was a small breakfast area with gorgeous raw wood furniture. In the middle of the room, Alyssa saw a bed covered with a Navajo blanket.

A bed.

A single bed.

One.

Past the bed, she saw a raised stone partition. And just past the partition was a sitting area, complete with a cozy couch, a wood-burning fireplace with a mantel clock over it, and a stack of piñon wood next to a door that stood open, revealing a rustic back patio.

On the left, opposite the bed, was a work area. A roomy desk and a comfortable chair. A flat-screen television was mounted on the wall above the desk, in the perfect position to be viewed from the bed.

All fabulously laid out and supremely decorated.

In fact, it lacked only one thing: another door.

It took a moment, but the import of that oversight finally keyed inside Alyssa's addled brain.

There was no door to another bedroom. This was it. This was the entire suite.

One room.

One bed.

And the couch wasn't even a fold-out. She could tell that much from here.

She turned around to face Chris, who still hadn't answered the question she now repeated. "Where the heck is the bedroom?"

"Ah," he said, looking as confused as she felt. "I think we may be standing in it."

"Suite," she said. "I thought you had a suite."

"I did. I mean, I do." He held up the key and the little paper envelope in which it had come. "It says so right here. Deluxe Junior Suite."

The bellman stepped into the open doorway behind Chris. "Is everything okay?"

"No problems," Chris said.

"Where's the bedroom?" Alyssa said at exactly the same time.

The bellman looked from one to the other. "Let me guess. You won't be wanting the bridal champagne and strawberries package."

Alyssa ran her fingers through her hair and scowled. "It's a great room. Honestly, one of the nicest I've ever seen. It's just that we're, um, not...you know." She cleared her throat. "We expected a suite."

The bellman looked at Chris, who shrugged. Then the bellman shrugged, as well, and Alyssa wondered if some sort of secret guy message had passed between the two of them. "The junior suite's an open room with distinct areas. The full suite and the celebrity suites have separate rooms, but I promise you this is one of our most popular floor plans."

He glanced hopefully at Alyssa, then frowned and cleared his throat. "Ah, it's popular with most of our guests, anyway."

Alyssa opened her mouth to ask about the possibility of moving them to another room. One with a bedroom. Emphasis on the *room* syllable. Then she shut it again. Because, hey, she'd invited herself along, and beggars couldn't be choosers, right? And the couch looked pretty comfortable.

She was, however, exceptionally glad that she'd packed a sweatshirt to wear over her pajama top. True, she'd spent more than her fair share of time with Chris on the couch beside her, and her curled up with her Sylvester pj bottoms and her Tweety tank top. But they'd only been friends then. Now they were—

Oh, dear Lord.

It was true. She and Chris had already crossed some invisible line. They'd put a toe across with that exceptional kiss, and then on this trip they'd somehow inched all the way over the line.

So what the hell was she supposed to do now?

Nothing, apparently, as there was nothing she could do. Nothing except ignore it. It wasn't as if she could travel back in time. Or turn off her hormones.

Or find another room to sleep in.

Except she could. Hadn't Russell offered to find her a room of her own? So all she needed to do was cross to the phone, pick it up and have the front desk connect her with Russell's room. She started to do exactly that as soon as the bellman backed out, thanking Chris for the generous tip, and apologizing again for the mis-understanding about the suite.

She stood watching Chris close the door, the handset cradled on her shoulder and her finger hovering over the button to dial the front desk.

She didn't push it. Instead she stood there, a gooey mass of indecision.

Chris moved toward her, then pulled out one of the kitchen chairs. He flipped it around and straddled it casually, looking for all the world like a guy without a single care. "You might want to wait until tomorrow," he said.

"What?" The word came out high-pitched and squeaky. Guilty.

"To ask Russell for a new room."

"I…" She hung up the phone. "Don't you think I should move?"

"Alyssa. How many times have you fallen asleep with your feet on my lap while we've been watching movies?"

She scowled. "Only when you insist we watch the boring ones."

"Why do you think I do that?" he said, then waggled his eyebrows in an overly exaggerated lecherous gesture.

She couldn't help it—she laughed. "Okay. Fine. I get that I'm being ridiculous. It's only that…"

He stood up and moved toward her, closing the distance between them in three long strides. "It's only what?"

"I…" She shook her head and forced a smile, because no way was she going to tell him what was really going on in her head. "Nothing. I guess I'm feeling guilty. About horning in on your room. You have a ton of work to do, and now I'm going to be in your way all the time. Not exactly what you bargained for."

"Hey," he said, taking her hand and sending little sparks of awareness zinging all through her. "Do you see me complaining?"

She swallowed, hoping she looked normal and that she'd have an actual, working voice when she opened her mouth. "You're too nice to complain."

"Remember that the next time you hear me yelling at the idiot who lives next door to me," he said, referring to the college freshman who lived on their floor and seemed to have mistaken their apartment building for a concert hall. He gave her hand a squeeze, then let go before turning around and heading toward the kitchen. As soon as his back was to her, she exhaled. She was treading water here, trying to keep from drowning, and she was seriously afraid that she was doing a piss-poor job of it.

What she needed was a game plan. A purpose. And what better place to look than oh, say, reality? *Professional* reality.

Feeling more grounded now that she had a plan, she began to look at the Holiday Guide that Chris had tossed on the tabletop. "There's stuff going on every night. A big party Christmas Eve, and there's caroling tonight," she said. "Marshmallows and sing-alongs around the fire."

"It will take a lot more than marshmallows to get me to sing in public," Chris said, returning to her side bearing two glasses of wine. "Look what I found in the wet bar."

"We have a wet bar?" she asked, then realized that what she'd assumed was an ornate credenza actually opened into a fully-stocked bar. Good. She needed a drink.

Or maybe not so good. At the moment, loose inhibitions sounded a little too delicious. Like a double-fudge banana split with extra cherries. Sinfully good, but so not good for you.

Around Chris, loose inhibitions fell firmly in the realm of banana splits. Not going there. Not going there…

Her eyes skimmed over the room to land on the bed, and her stomach did a little somersault.

So not going there.

Though she had to admit it was getting harder to remember *why* she wasn't going there.

Oh, yeah. Good friend. Utter ruination and destruction of valuable friendship. Complete descent into depression at the thought of losing him the same way she'd lost Bob. Couple that with his complete and utter financial irresponsibility, not to mention the fact that if he *was* going to be responsible, he'd have to travel so much he'd never be home.

Her new mantra? As they say on the BBC: don't shag your friends.

Too bad she'd suddenly found Chris deliciously shaggable.

"You're either saying a silent prayer to the wet-bar gods," Chris said, "or you've gone off somewhere else in your head. Tell me it wasn't the comment about my singing. I know it's mind-blowing, but I thought I had to actually produce a note or two before I fried circuits in the heads of people around me."

"You are *not* that bad," she said, laughing.

"Oh, believe me," he said. "I am."

"I've heard you sing," she said as he took a sip of his wine.

He almost sputtered, ending up in a coughing fit that left her awkwardly patting his back and muttering "Sorry! Sorry!"

"When?" he said, with the same edge of importance in his voice as if she'd told him an asteroid was about to plow into the resort. "When did I let you hear me sing?"

"Ah." She cleared her throat and hoped she wasn't blushing. At the same time, she really, really wished she hadn't brought this up. "Who can remember specifics?" she said, waving her hand as if the whole topic was of no importance. She held up the brochure. "Hot cocoa. Schnapps. Festive fun. Come on, let's go down."

"No way," he said, settling back in his chair and shaking his head. For a guy who usually presented such a laid-back persona, he appeared remarkably dug in.

"Well, suit yourself. It sounds like fun, though. I guess I'll just go alone."

She took a step for the door, only to be stopped by his short, curt "Alyssa."

She turned, looking at him with all the innocence she could muster. "Hmm?"

"Where did you hear me sing?"

Just any other conversation. This was just any other conversation.

"In the shower," she said, the words tripping fast over her tongue.

In front of her, Chris's eyes seemed to dance with amusement. "Really?" He propped his elbow on the back of the chair, then tucked his fist under his chin, as if he was settling in for a long and fascinating story. "I'm surprised I don't remember this. I'm pretty sure you seeing me in the shower is the kind of thing that would be forever burned in my memory. In Technicolor. And for a really long time."

"It was a few months ago, okay? I came over to your place to borrow a book—I don't even remember now." The reason she'd come over had been erased from her brain the moment she'd seen Chris's form behind the glass shower doors. "And I thought you said to come in, and so I did, and…"

She still didn't know what had possessed her to walk through Chris's apartment toward the bedroom. She'd heard the shower running, after all. But she'd gone. She'd taken one step, then another, with no certain plan and no certain purpose. Hell, it wasn't even as if she was looking to see him, because honestly, who showers with the bathroom door open? The whole point of a hot shower was to get all hot and steamy. But Chris had let the steam escape into the bedroom, and as she'd stood in his bedroom doorway and looked across the room toward the master bath, she'd had an absolutely phenomenal full-frontal view.

Whoa. Even now, months later, the memory was simply… *Whoa.*

She'd stayed there, frozen to the spot, her body turning warm and then cold and then warm again, and her throat tightening. His eyes had been closed, his face covered with soap, and as she'd gaped like some drunken spectator at a male strip club, he'd turned and put his face in the spray, giving her a delicious view of a tight, taut ass.

No doubt about it—from the waist down, the man was fine. Very fine.

For that matter, he was pretty fine from the waist up, too.

She'd started to back out, but then he'd started singing "Wake Me Up Before You Go-Go" by Wham! and his voice was just horrifying enough to bring a smile to her face, especially when he added a few choice dance moves to the song.

She'd stayed for the first verse, and was actually about to applaud when she realized what she was doing and caught herself before her hands came together.

She'd backtracked out of the apartment, run across the hall to her door and completely forgotten the reason she'd gone to Chris's apartment in the first place.

But she didn't forget the way he looked. To this day,

she could conjure that image anytime she liked. And in Technicolor, just like Chris had said.

"And I was singing in the shower?"

"Yeah," she said. "I mean, I only heard you," she lied, her cheeks burning from embarrassment. "It's not like I walked into your bathroom and took candid photos to post on the Internet or something."

"Thanks for that," he said, deadpan.

"The point is," she said firmly, trying to get their conversation back on track, "that your voice isn't as terrible as you say." That was another blatant lie. "And even if it is, so what? It's Christmas carols, not *American Idol*." She tried out a smile. "Please?"

She waited for him to answer, surprised that she really wanted him to say yes. She might be mortified by the memory, and still uncomfortable with sharing a room, but the idea of spending a fun holiday evening with Chris didn't stymie her at all. The only thing that would disturb her, in fact, was if he said no.

"I should work," he said, and she felt her heart sink. "But I'm zonked from the plane ride."

"So you'll come?" She told herself the giddy feeling stemmed only from the fact the caroling party sounded like fun. That, and the fact that they had moved on from the whole naked-in-the-shower debacle.

That wasn't true, though, and no matter how much she lied to herself she couldn't escape the truth: she wanted Chris. *Wanted him.*

She wasn't entirely sure why the feelings she'd for so long kept firmly buried had decided to rise to the surface tonight, but there was no denying the warm tingle of lust that bubbled in her veins.

A bubble she desperately needed to pop.

Because if she wasn't extremely careful, she was going to take advantage of the fact that they'd been thrown together in a suite with only one bed.

And that, she knew, she'd regret for the rest of her days.

8

"OKAY, group one! *Jingle bells! Jingle bells! Jingle all the way!* That's great. Keep going." The activities director—a type-A personality that Chris had already decided must be stopped—turned to the left side of the room. "And now group two, let's show them how it's done. *Jingle bells…*"

Chris leaned over to Alyssa. *"Someone smells—"*

She smacked him on the arm, and he mixed his howl with a laugh, earning them both an irritated scowl from Ms. Type-A.

Chris waved in apology, then signaled to Alyssa before standing and moving across the room to the double glass doors that opened onto a huge patio peppered with firepits and cozy chairs.

"Not your cuppa?" Alyssa asked, curling up in one of the chairs and holding her hands out toward the fire.

"I think I'm more of a sit-around-the-piano-while-someone-else-sings-'Hark-the-Herald-Angels' kind of guy."

"Yeah," she said. "Me, too." She made a face, her nose crinkling. "Sorry about dragging you down to that."

He laughed. "It's not your fault. I needed to get out and check out the hotel and the activities for my article." He frowned. "Though I may cut the resort a break and leave this little incident out. I think it deserves a passing comment on the blog, though," he added, making a quick note on his PDA.

"The tree's fabulous," she said.

He laughed. "Yeah, it's great. I'll mention that, too." Now that the check-in crowd had dissipated, they'd been able to get a good look at the tree, a towering fir that reached up three stories and was decorated in silver and blue. "Besides, I enjoyed the look of total mortification on your face when we sat down and she announced that we'd be doing a round-robin version of 'Jingle Bells.'"

Alyssa's cheeks bloomed red. "It was that obvious? Do you think Nancy noticed?" she asked, referring to Ms. Type-A.

"I'm positive she didn't." Alyssa hadn't been the only dumbstruck guest, and yet Ms. Type-A had barreled on with her plan for doling out the fun.

He frowned, realizing he wasn't exactly a prime example of holiday joy. "We could do our own round robin," he said.

"You'd sing?"

"Good point. No. How about we see if the staff can get us some sticks and marshmallows." He nodded toward the firepit. "You game?"

"I haven't roasted marshmallows since Girl Scout camp," she said. "No fireplace."

He nodded. His apartment didn't have a fireplace, either.

"Oh!" She bounced in her seat, leaning toward him, her eyes bright with excitement. "Maybe they have graham crackers and chocolate bars, too." He must have looked blank, because she continued. "S'mores! Don't tell me you've never had a s'more?"

He shook his head slowly, wondering what he'd missed out on. Considering Alyssa's level of little-girl-quality excitement, he was certain it was amazing. "Sorry. I've led a dull and sheltered existence."

"I guess so." She reached out and grabbed his hand, her expression serious, like a doctor speaking to a horribly injured patient. "But don't worry. We'll set you right."

Before he had a chance to wonder what he was getting into, she raised a hand and caught the attention of one of the staff. A tall guy in a crisp white shirt hurried over. "What can I do for you?"

"I have kind of a strange request," Alyssa said. "The kitchen wouldn't happen to have graham crackers and chocolate—"

"And marshmallows?" he asked, then grinned at Alyssa's delighted expression. "I think we've got just the thing."

He returned a few minutes later with plastic bags containing marshmallows, graham crackers and chocolate bars. "Oh, yeah," Alyssa said as she took them from him. "This is definitely a five-star resort." She turned to Chris as soon as the staff guy left. "Okay," she said. "Get ready to taste a little heaven."

Heaven, it turned out, was an understatement.

Chris's mind was completely distracted with everything involved in making the s'mores. As the chocolate melted over the graham cracker, he had a vision of Alyssa and melted chocolate. He tried to push the thought from his mind, really not needing to be dwelling on the thought of licking oozing chocolate off her smooth skin.

Then he dripped so much chocolate and sticky marshmallow goo onto his chin that he was certain he resembled a toddler eating his first piece of cake—which pretty much quelled his little sensual fantasies.

Or maybe not, he thought as Alyssa laughed, delighted, and reached over to brush an errant glob of marshmallow from his lips. Her eyes were dancing as she lifted her finger to her mouth and slowly licked off the confection. And while she may have meant the gesture as innocent, there was nothing innocent about Chris's reaction. He was hard as a rock, his erection straining against his jeans, and absolutely no way to hide it other than the dark.

"Delicious," she said.

"Yeah." His voice came out strained, desperate, and he had to fight the near-overwhelming urge to pull her close, bury his fingers in her hair and kiss her hard and deep.

"Chris? You okay?"

"Fine." Right then, he really couldn't manage more than single syllables, and he desperately, *frantically,* hoped she didn't realize the cause of his new tongue-tied nature.

"You want to be careful not to burn yourself," she said, focusing again on the marshmallows and the sticks. She jammed a marshmallow into the flames, all her attention on the fire. "I used to love to do this as a kid. Completely burn the marshmallow to a crisp. How about you?"

"Yeah," he said, still not trusting his voice. "Great." He needed to get out of here before he embarrassed them both. Either that or he needed to make a solid, definitive move in her direction.

At the moment, frankly, escape seemed easier.

Coward.

He drew in a breath and shifted. "Listen, it's getting on toward midnight, and I'm beat. I'm going to head back to the room."

"Oh." She put the stick down on the edge of the fireplace. "Well, okay. I'll come with you."

He started to tell her that wasn't necessary, then realized that he would be a complete idiot even to suggest such a thing. He had a hard-on for the woman— literally. And she wanted to go back to the room with him. Not after him. Not later, after she'd mingled with the crowd.

But with him, right then.

That was an opportunity he didn't intend to squander. "Right. Okay, then. Let's go."

He got up stiffly, thinking about things like editing and answering mail and changing the oil in his car. But that didn't work. Because the only thing he'd be editing would be the Max Dalton books, and Alyssa had worked her sweet, sexy way into that fantasy. As for the mail, he imagined a love letter from her, written in her round, feminine script.

And he had too vivid an imagination to turn off the alluring images of a naked Alyssa, her skin slick with oil as she pressed against him, their bodies gliding together, slick and hot and wet.

Okay, that really wasn't working.

He tried again to tone down his thoughts, this time reciting multiplication tables in his head.

He was up to the five-times table when they passed Ms. Type-A, who had moved the crowd on to "Jingle Bell Rock." And it was then that Chris discovered another reason he should have simply stayed put on the deck: Russell Starr, chatting with a cluster of guests outside the entrance to the bar, less than twenty feet from them.

Chris veered left, away from Russell and toward the main entrance. "Why don't we take the long way back to our room? It's such a fabulous night. We can probably see every star in the sky."

"Sure," she said, and he breathed a sigh of relief as she shifted slightly toward him. His relief was short-lived, because almost as quickly as she'd turned, she stopped. "Hang on. There's Russell."

Chris cursed silently, then turned to face Russell again. And, yeah, looking at the guy that Alyssa had come to New Mexico to seduce was a definite erection killer.

"I want to ask him to save a few minutes for me

tomorrow after the horseback-riding." She took a step in that direction, taking his hand as she did.

He didn't follow, and she stopped when the tension between their arms tightened.

"Chris?"

"Why don't we head on up? I'm sure you can mention it to him tomorrow."

She hesitated, then nodded. "You're probably right."

He exhaled, then took a step toward the exit. She followed, then stopped, and he knew for certain that he'd lost this round.

"Actually, no." She didn't meet Chris's eyes, but instead seemed to look everywhere but, even as her tongue flicked out to moisten her deep-red lips. Then she cocked her head back toward Russell, her cheeks blooming pink. "So, um, I just feel like if I want a business meeting, it's only fair to give him some notice. Doesn't feel right to yank his chain at the last minute." She squeezed his hand, letting go far too quickly for Chris's taste, then took a single step away from him.

Away from him and toward the enemy.

And that, Chris thought, truly sucked.

OH, DEAR Lord.

Alyssa was in trouble.

Big trouble.

Her mind drifted back to the outline of the erection she'd seen in Chris's jeans, and she amended the thought: *huge* trouble.

As for where her imagination was going—extrapolating what she'd seen of him that day in the shower and applying that memory to what she'd seen just now—well, that was too dangerous even to think about.

"Business," she muttered, ignoring the few passersby who shot her questioning looks. "Don't think about Chris. Think about the fact that you like to eat and have health benefits."

Right.

With a firm nod, she smoothed down her blouse, then crossed the room, a professional smile on her face.

Russell turned as she approached, and she saw the bloom of heat in his eyes. "Alyssa." He held out a hand, urging her toward the group. "I hope you've been enjoying your stay so far?"

"It's been great," she said. "The hotel is beautiful."

Russell pressed a hand against her back, easing her forward to subtly include her in the group. "Everyone, I'd like to introduce Alyssa Chambers. We went to high school together, but she doesn't hold those wild days against me." He introduced each person in turn, making Alyssa feel both welcome and special. "You met Mandy earlier," he added, indicating the blonde whom Alyssa remembered only too well.

"His default dinner date," Mandy said, then laughed. "But you'd better enjoy me while you have me," she said to Russell, a tease in her voice. "Barry's arriving tomorrow and then I'm all his."

"Mandy and my cousin Barry are engaged," Russell explained. "The women in my family have been taking turns playing escort to me over the last few weeks whether I like it or not." He shot Mandy a look of mock exasperation, making his soon-to-be in-law smile.

"He broke up with his girlfriend a few months ago," Mandy explained, then turned to Russell. "Oh, stop looking at me like that. It was all over the social pages, so I'm not saying anything that half the world doesn't already know."

"Mandy."

She held up her hands in surrender. "Fine. Fine." She smiled at Alyssa, and Alyssa took a step back, suddenly feeling much like a steak in a butcher's glass case must feel. "And what do you do?"

"I'm an attorney," Alyssa said. She tilted her head toward Russell. "Actually, that's why I came over just now. I wanted to see about scheduling a time to talk business with you."

He pressed a hand to his chest. "And here I thought you simply couldn't resist my charms."

She laughed, the reaction genuine. Despite being rich as Midas, Russell was as down-to-earth and nice as she remembered. "I won't deny you have ample charms," she said, teasing him right back. "But I'm a focused professional. I like to think that's one of *my* charms."

"Zing," Mandy said. "I like her, Russell." She took a step closer. "We're going over to Russell's room for drinks. He has a lodge on the far side of the complex. The view is amazing. Want to join us?"

"Oh, I couldn't," Alyssa said automatically, then mentally kicked herself, because that was exactly the kind of thing she *should* do. He was available. He liked her.

How much more perfect could it get?

A lot more perfect, a small voice in her head said.

She thought of Chris, and realized the little voice was right. The way his touch had made her tingle. The way she'd shivered when she'd seen his eyes on her as she'd licked the marshmallow off her fingertip. And the way she'd gone all warm and soft between her thighs when she'd realized he'd gone hard—and that it was her he was craving.

Just the memory alone was enough to have her saying her excuses to Russell and trying to gracefully extricate herself from the conversation.

She needed to be alone.

Hell, she needed a cold shower.

What was it they said about the best-laid plans?

She wasn't certain, but she knew that hers had gotten all messed up.

"I NEED help," Alyssa said into her phone.

At the other end of the line, Claire yawned. "Mom?"

"Claire! Wake up! It's me. Alyssa. I'm in trouble."

"Are you hurt?" Claire asked, immediately alert and worried. "Did you call the cops? Where are you?"

"I'm in the ladies' room by the lobby bar at Russell's hotel, and it's not that kind of trouble. Guy trouble."

"Ah," Claire said knowingly. "What's going on with Russell?"

"Nothing."

"Nothing?" Claire repeated. "Have you seen him?"

"I saw him. He invited me to his room. And made a point of letting me know he's single."

There was a pause at the other end of the line, and Alyssa was certain that Claire's forehead was creased in confusion and her lips were parted as she tried very hard to figure out exactly what she should say to that. "Uh, you want to run that by me again?"

Alyssa did.

"And you said no?" Claire's voice rose in total disbelief. "You actually turned down an invitation to the hotel owner's private suite?"

"I got the appointment, though. With Russell. About the job, I mean. We're going horseback-riding tomorrow, and then he said he could give me an hour. Whatever I need."

"I bet he did," Claire said. "Alyssa, what on earth were you thinking?"

Alyssa drew in a deep breath, then whispered, as if Chris could hear her all the way across the resort. "It's just that…"

"What?"

"I think I'm attracted to Chris."

"No!" Claire squealed. "That's awesome. You guys are totally cute together."

"No," Alyssa said. "No cute. Problem. Big, big problem."

"Why? Is he not interested back? I know he's never come on to you or anything, but I always assumed that was because he's shy. You know. Introverted writer

type. But you know what they say about still waters."
She managed to lace her voice with enough lascivious
tones that Alyssa felt her face warm.

"Oh, he's interested," Alyssa said. "But he's my
friend, Claire. Next to you, he's probably my best
friend."

"But that's perfect. You already know you guys get
along together. It couldn't get any better."

"I thought it made sense with Bob, and now he won't
even take my phone calls. I had to call his mom and ask
her to ask him to return my DVDs. And then he mailed
them to me—didn't even come by and drop them off."

"Chris isn't Bob."

"No," Alyssa agreed. "He's not." Bob had been solid
boyfriend material. An engineer at a local semicon-
ductor manufacturer, Bob was both solvent and fiscally
responsible. Nothing like Chris at all.

"Why can't Chris be a fling?" Claire asked. "You're
not attracted to Russell—fine, good, whatever. You're
insane, but whatever. And you are hot for Chris. He's
hot for you. You're in a hotel room together. You're both
over twenty-one. What's the problem?"

"You know what the problem is," Alyssa said.

"Bullshit. Not buying it. Maybe you started out
thinking that sex would get in the way of the friendship,
but guess what? It already has. It's in your head now,
and it's not going away."

It was a point that Alyssa had to concede. "So what
should I do? Walk into the hotel room and jump him?
I don't want him as more than a friend, Claire—I

don't." About that, she was standing firm. Chris's life-style drove her nuts from across the hall. If she was actually on the inside watching him run his life, she'd undoubtedly end up in a padded cell. "But I don't want to lose him as a friend, either."

"You could try talking to him."

Alyssa frowned. Considering she made her living negotiating deals with clients, opposing counsel and judges, the idea of actually sitting Chris down and talking to him was making her decidedly fidgety. "Maybe."

"Either that, or take a cold shower. Right now, though, I'm going back to sleep. Some of us have no sex life, and actually sleep during sleeping hours."

"How did your drink with Joe go?" Alyssa asked, both because she wanted to know and because Claire's problems deserved attention along with her own.

"Oh, there were sparks," Claire said. "It turned out…interesting. I'll tell you when I get back."

"Well, okay," Alyssa said. Joe wasn't her favorite person in the world, but if he was really who Claire wanted, she'd support her friend every step of the way.

After Claire hung up, Alyssa stood staring at her face in the bathroom mirror, trying to decide what to do. On the one hand, just the thought of a holiday fling was firing her senses. But there was still the downside wherein her life crashed and burned and she lost Chris forever.

Not exactly a decision to be made lightly, although being responsible and pragmatic was becoming more difficult the more she thought about it. Because the more she let Chris into her head, the more she wanted to get him naked.

Man, she had it bad.

Since she would probably do something stupid if she went straight back to the room, she headed instead for the bar. A seemingly endless loop of *Jeopardy!* was playing on one of the game-show networks, and she passed a pleasant two hours sipping rum-laced eggnog and wondering how those people managed to keep so many facts and figures in their heads. Impressive, she thought, especially considering that at the moment she was doing well to recall her room number.

Most likely, the *Jeopardy!* contestants weren't partaking of the holiday nog.

She frowned and blinked and realized that if she didn't stumble to her room now, the odds were good that she would end up sleeping on a couch in the lobby. Security would be called, Russell would be informed, and he would never in a million years trust his legal issues to a delinquent couch sleeper.

Which meant she had to go to the room she shared with Chris.

Chris, who was probably—she hoped—asleep.

She wondered if he slept in the nude.

The thought of Chris nude put an extra spring in her step…and then had her considering if maybe sleeping in the lobby wasn't such a bad idea after all.

"Alyssa, you're a mess."

She stopped in front of the door to their room, drew in a deep breath, and then slid the key card through the slot in the reader. The green light flashed and Alyssa pushed inside.

A fire burned in the fireplace, but other than that, the room was bathed in darkness, and a quick tinge of disappointment settled in her stomach.

Even though she was certain it was a bad idea, she'd still hoped to see Chris. Hoped to talk with him, have a drink with him.

And, yeah, maybe possibly ignore her inner naysayer.

She clenched her fists against the thought. *No.* Honestly, considering the state of mind she was in, it was for the best that Chris had crashed early.

Then again, according to the clock on the wall, it was after two in the morning. Not so early after all.

Moving silently, she headed for the bathroom, planning to change quickly and quietly into pjs. She found the note he'd left on the mirror right away, and as she skimmed it, the bubble of another fantasy she'd been refusing to acknowledge burst with a pop: *A—you take the bed, I'll crash on the couch—C.*

So much for sharing a bed with the man. Even if nothing happened between them, she had to admit to the secret anticipation of sleeping next to him. Just the possibility of such proximity seemed undeniably erotic, and the wash of disappointment that now crashed over her was frustrating her. She had no business being disappointed, not where Chris and thoughts of sex were concerned.

The bathroom was stocked with a variety of moisturizers and soaps, shampoos and conditioners, and she poked around the drawers and baskets, curious what kind of goodies a first-rate spa hotel offered its guests.

She found a binder on a bamboo table next to the tub that actually outlined the room features, and she flipped idly through it, noting that the hotel had a manicurist who would come to your room, in addition to a massage therapist and even a detox consultant.

But what really caught her eye was the reference to the fact that each Deluxe Junior Suite had a hot tub on the back patio.

Now *that* was some very interesting information. Especially since at the moment, Alyssa could think of very little more appealing than sitting in bubbling hot water and looking at the stars. Well, she corrected, she couldn't think of anything more appealing that she could do by herself.

Quietly, she stripped off her clothes, then slipped into one of the robes the hotel had conveniently hung in the little closet behind the bathroom door. She turned off the light, then stepped out into the room, walking softly so she wouldn't wake Chris.

As she passed the couch, she peered to the right, then saw the lump under the Navajo blanket. She tiptoed across the suite, then pushed carefully out onto the back patio. The moon had disappeared behind a cloud, casting the patio in nothing but dark shadows. She found a switch for a porchlight, but decided not to use it. She could smell the water from the hot tub, could hear it bubbling to the left, and after her eyes adjusted, she could see the dim light of the moon reflecting on the frothy ripples of water.

Perfect.

She took a step toward it, opening the robe as she moved, then let it slip off her shoulders. It fell to the wooden deck, pooling around her ankles as her body tightened, gooseflesh rising from the chill night air. One more step, and then she froze as the familiar voice eased around her, warm and soft and intimate.

"Alyssa," Chris said. "You're even more beautiful than I imagined."

9

CHRIS had to be dreaming. There was simply no other explanation for the fact that he'd been drowning his sorrows in the hot tub, and fantasizing what he would do if Alyssa dumped Russell and headed back home to him. How he would tell her that he wanted to touch her. Wanted to kiss her.

Wanted *her.*

And now here she was.

Clearly an illusion.

Except it wasn't.

That was a flesh-and-blood woman there. Beautiful, and perfect. With soft curves and skin that seemed to glow in the light from the moon that was only now peeking out from behind the clouds, as if the moon itself wanted nothing more than to see her beauty, as well.

God, I've become such a sap.

Maybe that's what half an hour in a hot tub thinking about a woman he couldn't have did to a man. And now that said woman stood naked in front of him, the circuits in his brain were completely fried, and everything he'd told himself he would say had completely evaporated from his head.

In fairness, she looked a bit rattled herself, but Chris had a feeling that probably had a lot to do with finding herself standing naked before him.

"Come into the water." He said the only thing that came to mind.

Her hand was over her crotch, her arm pressed across her breasts. "What?" her voice came out high and squeaky. The voice of a woman who was more than a little freaked out.

"You came out here because you wanted a soak in the hot tub, right? So get in. Once you're under the water, I won't be able to see a thing."

"You can see something now," she said.

He decided not to mention how exceptional his current view was. "I'm closing my eyes. Come on, Alyssa. Join me."

He closed his eyes and held his breath, waiting for her to make her decision. Then he heard it. The sound of her footsteps on the deck, the subtle shift in the water as she stepped down, then sank beneath the bubbles.

She'd actually done it. She'd joined him and brought his own personal fantasy that much closer to reality.

"I'm in," she said, her voice little more than a whisper.

"I know," he said, then opened his eyes. She was right there, pressed against the far side of the tub, sitting at a slant so that the water came up to her shoulders, every bit of her breasts hidden beneath the water.

"I, uh, thought you were asleep."

He shook his head. "Nope. Just waiting. Thinking."

"Oh." She drew her hand through the water as if scooping up bubbles. "What were you thinking about?"

He drew in a breath and told himself it was now or never. He could either get out of the water, go inside and keep his distance for the rest of the week, or he could try to get some traction here.

The decision was easy, because he wanted her more than he could ever remember wanting anything. The execution, however, was hard.

"Chris? Did you fall asleep on me?"

"I was thinking about you," he blurted, before he could stop himself.

Her voice came out on a breath. "Oh."

"Did you get your meeting?"

"Yeah. Tomorrow, after our trail ride. He, um, invited me to his room just now. Guess he's having a small party."

"You didn't stay." He spoke calmly, matter-of-factly. Inside, however, he was doing a cheer.

"No," she said. "Actually I didn't even go. I decided to come back here. Well," she added with a small laugh, "I had a few drinks in the bar first." She drew in a breath and then looked across the tub at him, her eyes boring straight into his. "I think I'm glad I did."

He slid off the seat and stepped to the middle of the pool, his movement cutting off her words.

"Chris, what are you doing?"

"Do you really want me to tell you?" he asked, reaching out to put his hand on her knee.

She flinched, but didn't pull away. Instead she sat very still, her breathing ragged, her teeth grazing her lower lip. "Please. Don't do this."

"Don't do what?"

She gestured between them. "This." Her voice was low, breathy. "I don't think we should—"

"I do," he said. He put his other hand on her other knee, biting back a smile of amusement at the way she kept her legs pressed so tightly together.

"Why exactly were you glad of those drinks?" he asked.

"Chris. Please."

"I had three glasses of Scotch, myself. I'm glad I did, too."

"Oh?" Her voice seemed small, far away. "Why?"

"Courage," he said, then pressed gently on her knees, easing them apart. At first, he felt only resistance, then she relaxed, drawing in a slow breath as he spread her knees, easing himself inside so that her thighs pressed against his ribcage. Under the water, his cock had sprung to attention, but right then, that wasn't the goal. Eventually, yeah. Eventually, he wanted to bury himself deep inside her. Wanted to lose himself inside her and feel her tremble around him as she came.

Right then, though, he craved only the feel of her lips upon his and the sweet surrender of everything she'd been holding back.

"Me, too," she whispered. "Courage, I mean."

"Did it work?" he asked, easing closer still.

"I'm not sure."

"Let's find out."

Before he could talk himself out of it, he leaned forward, brushing his lips softly against hers. He waited for her to pull away, absolutely certain she was going to put the brakes on this and leave him alone in the tub nursing a fourth glass of Scotch.

It really was the season of miracles, though, because she didn't pull away. On the contrary, she released a low, breathy moan, so sweet and needy that he got even harder, though how his body managed that, he'd probably never know.

"Alyssa?"

"A fling," she said, her voice heavy with desire.

"Whatever you say." Right then, he'd agree with her about anything.

"Some friends do that, right?"

He kissed her throat as she talked, enjoying the little moans that peppered her words.

"They have flings, I mean, but they're still friends."

"Best friends," he said, sliding his hands along the insides of her thighs. She trembled under his touch, and he felt powerful. Alive.

He felt like Max Dalton, a man who knew what he wanted and took it.

"Chris? I—Oh, God, that feels good—it's just that I think we need to be clear. We both need to understand what—"

"Alyssa?"

"Yes?"

He pulled back, looking at her face, at the passion

clouding her sharp eyes. "Turn off the lawyer and kiss me."

She stayed perfectly still for one beat, then another. Then desire flashed and she pulled him closer, crushing her mouth to his and giving him everything he'd ever wanted in the form of one hot, passionate kiss. Lips crushed, teeth nipping. Nothing but desire and heat and need until she pulled back, her breath coming fast and furious, matching his all the way.

Thank God. He moved in again, this time claiming her mouth with a soft tenderness. With his tongue he eased her lips open, then delved inside, exploring, tasting, *taking.*

She'd said that she'd gone to the bar, and he could taste the rum, a sweet holiday flavor that he wanted to devour along with every inch of her.

His body was tense from the pressure of holding back, but he didn't want to rush. Not now. Not with her.

He wanted to savor. Wanted to feel. Wanted to burn every single moment between them into his mind so that he could recall every scent, every sensation, at a moment's notice.

She wanted a fling, and for now that was fine. For now, that was just great. He'd give her the best damn fling she'd ever had.

His fingers wove through her hair, his palms curved and pressed to her scalp as if the more he held on, the more real this would become. Because, despite tasting her—feeling her—he still couldn't believe he had her.

And yet he did. She was right there in his arms, her

mouth moving under his, and when he backed off into the center of the tub, she came with him, both of them surrounded by warm, pulsating water.

"Turn around," he whispered, not waiting for her to respond, but shifting her himself, pressing her back against him so that the curve of her rear teased his erection. He pressed his mouth against her neck, one arm around her waist, keeping her close, the other hand sliding over her silky, wet skin. He found her nipple, and he took the bud in his hand, rolling it between his thumb and forefinger until he felt her breathing hitch and her hips swivel, as though searching for satisfaction.

He nipped her shoulder and whispered for her to wait, to just wait, because if it was satisfaction she wanted, he intended to provide that in spades.

His hand slipped down, the warm, bubbling water magnifying every sensation. His fingers caressed soft curls and he curled his index finger, molding himself to the shape of her.

In his arms, she moaned, then shifted, the movement opening her legs and giving him better access. "Alyssa," he murmured, and when her whispered "Please" drifted back to him, he was certain he was going to lose it right there.

He wasn't about to deny her, though, and he stroked her, moaning himself when he felt how slippery she was against his fingers. He slid inside her, closing his eyes as her muscles clenched tight around him, then sliding out and driving them both crazy as he did so.

Slowly, he teased her clit. Playing and dipping, finding a rhythm from the way she moved against him, the soft pressure of her rear taking him to the very brink.

"Come," he whispered, his fingers determined, and his tongue laving the curve of her ear. "Come for me."

A shudder passed through her, and she swallowed a cry. Her knees gave out, and then she sank into the water, limp. He eased her toward him, then settled them both on one of the hot-tub seats on the far side.

"Chris," she murmured, clinging to him. "Wow."

"Wow, indeed," he said, not even trying to hide his smile. "We should have done that a long time ago."

WE SHOULD have done that a long time ago.

His words echoed through her head, and Alyssa couldn't deny them. Didn't want to deny them.

And yet, dammit, she couldn't help but fear she'd let lust and chemistry drive her to do a stupid thing.

But how stupid could it be when Chris was right beside her, naked and gorgeous and looking at her as though she was the only woman on the face of the earth?

"Don't make me regret this," she whispered.

"Never," he said, and this time when his mouth closed over hers, his hand slipped down to cup her breast, covering her nipple, a rock-hard pebble that left absolutely no question but that she wanted this. And when he stroked it she couldn't prevent the gasp of pure, lusty delight that escaped her even as she arched her back, instinctively giving him better access.

The motion lifted her breasts partly out of the water, and she saw the heat in his eye before he closed his mouth over her other breast, the one that had so far lagged in attention. He suckled, his tongue doing to that nipple what his finger was doing to the other, and the combination wreaking absolute havoc on the rest of her body.

She squirmed, trying to find some satisfaction, wanting him to touch her elsewhere, everywhere, but he wasn't, not yet, and she didn't want to ask, because as soon as she asked, she knew he would comply, and the truth was she wanted the sweet torment to continue. Wanted to enjoy the way he discovered her body.

And, yeah, she wanted to make it last.

He drew her nipple in, suckling harder and tighter, and a hot wire of desire seemed to shoot through her core, connecting his tongue on her breast all the way to her clit. She heard herself moan and her fingers twitched. In her mind, she begged for him to touch her, and she feared—really feared—that she'd be unable to keep her promise to herself not to lead him, not to tell him, but simply to go with the flow.

She realized soon enough that she should have had more trust. Chris knew her, after all, and it only made sense that he would know her body, as well, instantly and instinctively.

Even while his mouth stayed on her breast, one hand pressed against the small of her back, holding her in place. Her own fingers were curled in his hair, pulling him closer, holding him steady, keeping him *right there* in case he should get other ideas. And all the while, his other hand abandoned its mission to deliver sweet torment to her nipple, and started tracing a path down beneath the water.

His fingers glided over her smooth skin, and she tensed as he eased near her belly button, then lower still, finally sliding into her slick core. His fingers found her clit and he played her mercilessly, his fingers dancing and stroking, making her body tremble as she came right up to the edge, but never quite crossed it.

"Do you like that?" he whispered.

"Yes," she whispered, in what had to be the understatement of the year.

"Me, too."

All too soon, though, he pulled his hand away, and though she whimpered, he showed no mercy. "Shh," he said, then turned her around again so that her back was pressed against him, the hard length of him teasing her rear, and his hands tight on her breasts.

"What are you—"

She didn't have to continue with the question, because it became all too clear what he was doing, and damned if it didn't feel amazing.

He'd maneuvered them both so that the jet from the hot tub spurted out in a hard stream right between her spread legs. And as the water teased her, his hands stroked her breasts and his tongue danced over her ear.

Her senses were bombarded, the pleasure so intense it was almost painful, and she squirmed, trying to get away. He was having none of it, though, and kept a firm hand, keeping her right there, unmoving, a prisoner to the most erotic of punishments.

She drew in a lungful of air as she climbed toward the orgasm, feeling it fill and pull her, playing with and teasing her.

And then, as if she'd fallen from the mountains themselves, she felt herself go over, her whole body trembling in his hands, his clever fingers taking the place of the jet stream and making the sensation last longer and longer until she was positive she would absolutely melt from pleasure.

"Don't let go of me," she murmured. "I'll sink under and you'll have to fish me out in the morning."

"I'm not about to let you go," he said, his voice so full of promise that she trembled again in his arms. "Can you walk?"

"Maybe next century," she said.

"Then hold on to my neck."

He picked her up and stepped out of the tub. She drew in a sharp breath, the shock of the freezing air against her overheated skin like a thousand needles poking and prodding.

He must have been as cold as she was, but he didn't complain, simply grabbed two of the fluffy towels the resort kept by the tub then eased inside. He dried her off, then slid her gently into the bed, the sheet, comforter and Navajo blanket covering her for warmth.

She snuggled down further, then watched him, realizing for the first time how muscular his body was. She'd seen him before, that clandestine time in the shower, but up close was so much better than that sneak peek had been.

She knew he biked regularly, and she seemed to recall him mentioning swimming laps, but she hadn't known how exquisite the end result had turned out to be. And it was amazing. Right then, looking at him as he added logs to the already burning fire, she had the distinct impression that he was a god. Or one of the mortals that a god had sculpted.

And when he turned to her and smiled, he seemed even more beautiful still. "Hey," he said, sliding under the covers with her. "Mind if I join you?"

"I think I'd be irritated if you didn't." She propped herself up on her side. "I've managed to get pretty warm here, but you were out there a lot longer than I was. I bet you're still chilled."

"Freezing," he said.

"Want me to try and warm you up?"

"I can't think of anything I want more."

"Good," she said, then shifted so that she straddled him and the blankets covered them both. The weight of the covers pressed down on her, and she went with it, dropping down so that her chest was pressed against his, her legs spread, and his erection teasing between them.

"Keep that up, and you're going to drive me insane," he said.

"What?" she asked innocently, sliding down so that her core rubbed ever so slightly against him. "That?"

"Vixen," he said. "I always knew those Tweety Bird pjs hid a true vixen."

She nipped him gently on the chin. "And proud of it."

She trailed kisses up his jaw, finishing with a gentle tug on his earlobe. "But I can't have you thinking I'm the kind of girl who tortures perfectly innocent men."

Slowly, she inched down until her fingers could comfortably reach him. He felt like velvet-covered steel, and she closed her eyes, imagining him inside her. Filling her.

"Careful," he said, his voice raw. "Do that too much, and we'll miss the main event."

"Yeah?" She liked the sound of that. Liked knowing she could take him there, so close, and that now she could give him what they both so desperately wanted.

She slid down, pushing the covers as she went, wanting to explore every inch of him and drive him to the brink in the process. Slowly, she trailed her fingertips up his legs, her eyes closed as she listened to the sounds he made, low groans of pleasure and surprise, and the power of knowing that she made him feel that way—that she was making him want more—made the desire inside her twist and curve, demanding a satisfaction she wasn't quite ready to give.

She followed the path of her fingers with her mouth, trailing the tip of her tongue up the inside of his thighs, then cupping his balls and watching in delighted fascination as he arched with need, his cock twitching as if begging her to finish this. *Soon,* she thought, then eased close to taste him.

She flicked the tip of her tongue over the end of his

shaft, then drew her attention down, laving him like a lollipop while he whispered her name, warning her that he couldn't last much longer. The truth was, she really couldn't, either. "Do you have any condoms?"

He did, thank God, and she scooted quickly out of bed to retrieve one, then ran back and got two more, just in case. She tossed the extra packets on the bed, then used her teeth to rip open the little foil square. Her hands were shaking and she couldn't manage to unroll the thing, which was somewhat mortifying, but Chris just laughed and took care of that little detail for her. She bit back a laugh of her own, then pressed a kiss to his lips. He really was the most thoughtful guy.

"Alyssa," he said, this time without a hint of a laugh in his voice. "Now."

Her skin flushed merely from the heat in his voice, and when his hands closed on her hips, she felt the electric shock of his touch through every inch of her body. She rose up on her knees, then lowered herself, so wet that she took him in immediately, so tight that he moaned and arched up to meet her.

She leaned back, riding him, even as his finger eased forward, teasing her clit as she took him in and out, deeper and harder. She closed her eyes, her thoughts evaporating, leaving nothing but colors and sensations and the delicious scent of sex as the world seemed to explode around her, her own release coming only moments before he groaned and lost himself inside her.

She collapsed against him, urged down by his arms

pulling at her, then easing her close against him, her head fitting perfectly on his chest, his arm curled protectively around her.

"Wow," he said.

"Definitely wow," she agreed.

"So. Want to do it again?"

She laughed, then rolled over to look at his face. "Hell yes. You?"

"Absolutely." He kissed her hard. "A moment to recharge?"

"Television?"

"Seems appropriate," he said, grappling for the remote.

"Don't even think you get to be in charge of that thing," she said. "We are not watching sports after sex."

"Sports after sex is a time-honored tradition," he insisted. "Like a cigarette."

"We don't smoke," she said, then leaned across him. "So give me the remote."

"Try and get it," he said, scooting away from her.

"Hey! Wait a second."

"See?" he said. "See? This is how it starts. First sex. Then a power struggle for the remote. We're well on our way to coupledom. And just think, we've been fighting about the remote for years, so we already have a head start."

Coupledom.

The word echoed in her head, killing her smile. She grabbed the pillow and scooted back, looking in the other direction when Chris caught her eye.

"Uh-oh," he said. "What is it?"

"We said fling, remember? In the hot tub. You promised a fling. Not coupledom."

"Right," he said, his expression a cross between concern and amusement.

"There are rules, Chris. There have to be rules."

"Shall we draw up a contract, counselor?"

She sighed and gave him a light smack on the shoulder. "We just need to be clear. We're friends. Friends who sleep together. But it's not a relationship."

"I know," he said. "I get it. But why?"

"I don't think it's a good idea for friends to become a couple."

"Ah," he said, leaning back and nodding knowingly.

She exhaled in relief, pleased he understood.

"So you'd rather date someone you don't really get along with that well?"

"No, I—"

"Someone like Russell?"

He was looking at her with such certainty that she couldn't help but blush. "Chris, I didn't mean—"

"It's okay," he said. "I overheard you and Claire talking. I should have told you that a long time ago. I don't usually make a practice of eavesdropping."

"Oh." Fingers of mortification crept near her. He'd known she wanted to seduce Russell. Which, considering she'd realized that any spark there might have been with Russell had long ago faded, seemed particularly ironic. "I'm not interested in him," she said. "There's nothing between me and Russell and there isn't going to be. You should know that, considering…well, considering this."

"Really?" He shifted, looking at her with interest. "That's good to know. But it still leaves open the question of why friends can't be couples."

"You saw what happened with Bob," she said.

"I did," he agreed. "And here's a news flash for you. I'm not Bob."

Frustrated, she ran her hands through her hair. "This isn't a negotiation. Those are my terms. Take them or leave them."

"A fling," he said. "And that's it."

"That's the deal."

He stuck out his hand and nodded. "All right, then. We have a contract."

She shook, and as she did, he tugged her close, then kissed her so long and so hard she was certain her toes would melt. "About that television break," he said.

"Yeah?"

"Suddenly I'm not so interested anymore."

10

CHRIS WOKE to the delicious sight of Alyssa bending over him, looking so fresh and perfect he was certain she'd been awake for hours. She was wearing that same, sexy Starr Resort bathrobe, and it gaped open to reveal the perfect curve of her breast. "Hey, sleepyhead. You want orange juice or coffee?"

"What?" he asked stupidly. "Coffee. Desperately, coffee."

"Sit up," she ordered, then smoothed the comforter on his lap when he complied.

She crossed the room to the kitchen area, then returned moments later with a tray topped with French toast, sliced strawberries, bacon and a tall glass of frothy orange juice next to a steaming mug of coffee.

"What's this?"

"Breakfast," she said, easing the tray onto his lap, then settling carefully on the bed beside him. "I slaved for hours over a hot room-service menu."

"Did you?"

"The torture. Honestly, I almost got a paper cut."

"The sacrifices we make for love." The moment the

word was out of his mouth, he regretted it. He'd told her he loved her dozens of times, but the context had always been as a friend.

Now he held his breath, terrified she'd bolt. She didn't. Instead she leaned in, brushed a kiss across his lips and whispered, "For the friends we love."

She snatched a piece of his bacon, then slid off the bed and moved to his laptop, which she tapped with the tip of her index finger. "Eat," she said. "And then I want your ass in this chair and your fingers on these keys. You're supposed to be writing, remember? And I have a feeling I've turned out to be a little more of a distraction than you'd anticipated."

He grinned at her. "Would you believe me if I said I didn't mind?"

"*I* mind," she said. "You have a manuscript to finish. Not to mention the article about this resort. And I don't want to be the reason you can't make the rent in January."

The smile faded on his lips. "You know, it's not as if the landlord is ready to evict me. It's not like my power's ever been cut off. And I have no creditors pounding at my door."

She pressed her lips together, then nodded. "Right. You're right. And it's really none of my business."

He fought the urge to roll his eyes. Because as much as he wished she'd lay off his lifestyle, he also did want it to be her business. He wanted it to be *their* business.

At the moment, though, she was right. Not about his rent, he had that covered through May, and he had a trip lined up in February and the money from that gig would cover him for a few months after that. But he did need to get his book finished, or else he'd not only suffer the wrath of Lil, but he might miss a window of opportunity for selling the thing.

"All right," he conceded. "Work it is," he said. "What are you going to do until we meet Russell to ride the trail?"

"Research," she said. "If I'm going to meet with Russell after our trail ride, then I need to have a solid feel for his corporate structure." She glanced at her watch. "I made an appointment with the concierge for nine."

He glanced at the clock on the bedside table. "So you still have some time before you need to go, right?"

"Yeah." She narrowed her eyes in suspicion. "Why?"

He took another bite of French toast, then pushed the tray away. "No particular reason. I was just hoping you could help me out."

"Help you out?" Her hands went to her hips, school-mistress style. Apparently, she was buying none of this. "Didn't I just tell you that you need to get your writing chops in gear?"

"That's what I need help with. A little Dalton research."

"Oh." He watched uncertainty flicker over her face. Her desire to help him out warring with that little niggle of certainty that he was playing games.

Smart girl.

"What kind of research?"

"Come here," he said, "and I'll show you."

"Chris…"

He held up his hands in mock surrender. "Hey, is it my fault that Natalia and Dalton are about to have a romantic interlude in a remote mountain cabin? You want me to get the details right, don't you?"

She stood there, passion warring with responsibility.

"Alyssa," he said, "I'm a man in serious need of assistance."

Her lips curved into a grin, and she eased toward him, then slipped one knee onto the bed. "Yeah, well, I'd hate for people to think I don't support the arts."

"Exactly," he said.

"So, um, how exactly can I help you out?"

He moved the tray off his lap, then reached out to untie the belt of her robe. "I'll show you," he said, then slid his hand inside, his palm cupping the curve of her waist even as she closed her eyes and arched back, sighing.

The clock chimed eight o'clock. "I need to be downstairs soon," she whispered, but made no move to pull away.

"Do you?" he murmured, easing the robe off her shoulder to reveal her smooth bare skin. "In that case, I guess we'll have to work fast."

AT FIFTY DEGREES, the afternoon was unseasonably warm, and Alyssa peeled herself out of the down-filled parka she'd worn and tied the arms around her waist, trying very hard not to lose her balance and fall off Old Earl in the process.

The horse, as gentle as the wrangler had promised, seemed to realize that she was new to riding and slowed his pace. She murmured a thank-you and held on tightly with her knees as she patted his soft neck.

Ahead of her, Chris was riding alongside Ed, the cowboy who was leading them, and Chris looked just as comfortable as the cowhand did. It was a side of Chris she'd never seen before, and it made her realize that despite the fact that they'd been close for years, there was still a lot of unexplored territory.

A vision of him naked popped into her head and she remembered the pleasure of doing exactly that: exploring every single inch of him.

In the meantime, though, she had to admit she was content to explore the trails, and she was absurdly grateful that Russell hadn't been able to join them after all.

He'd left a message with the concierge explaining that something had come up, and asking if Alyssa minded if her meeting got bumped back by another two hours. At the time, she'd been a little miffed, but now she wouldn't trade the time with Chris for anything.

"This is where we'll stop the groups for cowboy breakfasts," Ed said as Alyssa's horse eased up beside him. The cowhand took the reins, and she dismounted, then looked over at Chris, who was watching her intently. He caught her gaze, then smiled before turning away and looking out over the mountains.

"Hey. You okay?"

"I'm great," he said, squeezing her hand. "I'm just in awe." He nodded toward the snowcapped mountains, now sparkling in the sun like jewels. "I've been all over the world, and sometimes I forget how much beauty there is in my own backyard." He shifted slightly and stroked her cheek. "Or just across the hall."

She eased close and put her head on his shoulder, sighing as his arm went around her waist as casually as if he'd held her that way every day for the last two years. "I'm glad I came," she whispered.

"So am I," he said, then brushed his fingertip over her nose. "Right now, the only thing that would make this moment better is to be alone."

She laughed. "Yeah, well, we have a chaperone."

He flashed a wicked grin, then kissed her forehead before moving away toward Ed. She saw them put their heads together, and then after a moment, Ed slapped him on the back, mounted his horse and took off down the trail the way they'd come.

"What did you do?" she asked when he came back to her.

"I explained that three was a crowd."

"And he just left? What about the horses? What if they decide to do…whatever it is horses do?"

Chris looked over at the two remaining horses who were standing lazily around, their muzzles dipping experimentally to the ground trying to find tasty tidbits despite the light frost. "Yeah, they look about ready to riot."

She cocked her head and stared until he gave in.

"Kidding," he said. "I simply explained that I knew how to ride before I could walk, and that I'd make sure the four of us got back to the resort safe and sound."

"He believed you?" she asked, picking her way over some scrubby grass toward a large, flat boulder that looked like the perfect place to sit and take in the view.

"Why wouldn't he? It's true."

"Really?" She knew he'd grown up in a small Texas town, but she'd never considered the possibility of horses.

"It's been a handy skill, actually. I've ridden pack mules in Afghanistan and camels in Egypt. But I got my start on Silver."

"Hi-ho, Silver?"

"My dad was a Lone Ranger fan," he said.

"Why Afghanistan?" she asked, as he settled down on the rock next to her. She lay back, looking at the clouds and the clear sky, her head resting in the crook of his arm. "I thought you wrote about resort destinations."

"Now. When I first got my journalism degree, I was a stringer for one of the wire services, and I did a lot of foreign coverage. That's part of the reason why I went freelance. I wanted more control over when and where I travel."

She rolled over to face him. "And now? How much control do you have now?"

He shrugged. "A lot. I've got a good relationship

with *Tourist and Travel.* And I pretty much travel when I want and where I want."

"Then why don't you travel more? Steadily, I mean, instead of waiting months and then bunching a bunch of trips up together?"

He laughed. "Trying to get rid of me?"

"Not hardly. But, well…"

"The money," he said dully.

"I'm sorry," she said, sitting up. "But wouldn't you make more if you kept at it steadily?"

"Yeah," he said. "I would."

"Well, that's the thing. I just don't get it. You're smart and talented and you're living like you're still in college. An apartment, no car, you barely own furniture."

"You live in an apartment."

"I'm saving twenty percent down."

"Maybe I don't want a house."

The very idea baffled her. "Well, okay, maybe. But you still have to want—"

"What?"

"To know the world isn't going to be yanked out from under you one day." She pressed her fingertips to her temples and turned away, amazed that had come out like that.

"Your dad," he said simply. She'd told Chris about her childhood, of course. How could she not share with her best friend? "I'm not him," Chris said.

"I know," she said. "I do. But I look at you, and I worry."

He pressed a fingertip to her lips. "I love that you worry. It makes me feel special."

"You are." The words came out hoarse, and she fought back tears that were bubbling up inexplicably, as if they had to come to the party once her family drama had been dragged to the forefront.

He pressed a soft kiss to the corner of her lips. "I liked waking up next to you," he said.

"Me, too," she admitted. "But part of me is afraid we made a huge mistake."

"Not possible."

"Chris, I'm serious," she said, her finger stroking the silver of the friendship bracelet he'd bought her. "We've changed everything."

"Is that bad?"

"I put on makeup for you," she said abruptly. "I actually got showered and completely dressed this morning while you were still asleep."

"Ah," he said, then looked back over the mountain range, as if the way to deal with her capriciousness was hidden out there in the rugged peaks. "Um, is that a problem? Personally, I thought you looked damn good."

"Yes, it's a problem," she said, desperate for him to understand just how deep this makeup issue ran. "I put on makeup even though you've seen me hundreds of time with no makeup, ratty clothes and hair I hadn't bothered to brush because I'd been planning on a lazy Saturday in front of the television watching *American Movie Classics*. Never mind that you've seen me covered with paint and caulk from that time I decided my bathroom needed to be repainted right that very day."

"I have to admit you looked pretty cute with that caulk on your nose."

"Dammit, Chris, you're my best friend. I don't want that to change."

"Should we have put makeup in our contract?"

She tilted her head back and released a mock scream, but his mouth against hers made it catch in her throat. His tongue slid in, and her body responded instantly, reaching for him, wanting him, and totally unable to have him at the moment because she was wearing far too many clothes and they were lying on a rock in the middle of a cattle trail.

He pulled away, his hands on the rock on either side of her, a cocky grin on his face that she would have begrudged him if it wasn't so well-deserved. "Nothing's changed, Alyssa. We're still us. You and me, Chris and Alyssa."

"I know, but—"

He silenced her with another kiss, this one quick and businesslike. "Did you ever consider that maybe it wasn't a morning makeup thing, but maybe it was you wanting to feel like it was still that first night? I mean, Alyssa, we'd made love for the first time and it was amazing. I know I didn't want it to end. So maybe it wasn't about getting up and getting dressed before me. Maybe it was about wanting to feel sexy."

"I don't—"

He brushed her face. "For the record, I think you're sexy as hell even without makeup. You have six freckles on your nose that I can only see when your skin's bare. They're pretty sexy freckles."

She laughed, feeling utterly foolish. Because this was Chris, and he could always make her feel better. Then she reached up and gripped the back of his head, pulling him down for a hard, firm kiss. "About our fling agreement?"

"Yeah?"

"I think it's time to get back to the resort," she said. "I feel the need to enforce a few key provisions of our contract."

As FAR AS Alyssa was concerned, she would take riding Chris over riding a horse any day of the week. She straddled him, their bodies connected, and the control she had from being on top was almost as much of an aphrodisiac as the man himself.

Almost.

She rocked slowly at first, finding a rhythm as the pressure inside her built and built, nice and slow, like a gathering thunderstorm.

Beneath her, Chris's eyes were open, and he watched her, the heat she saw on his face shooting through her, making her wet, and when she couldn't stand it any longer she took his hand and moved his fingers in time with her thrusts, showing him how she wanted to be stroked. Not that he needed encouragement. She'd already discovered that Chris had magic fingers, and as he worked his magic on her she felt her breasts harden, her thighs tremble.

The room was silent except for the sound of sex, and their own soundtrack made the moment that much more erotic.

Her muscles tightened, drawing him in deeper, harder, and she kept the rhythm, listening to his soft voice urging her to come for him, to come with him, and then she did, and the world exploded and she collapsed against him, her body tingling and damp. She lay there, doing little more than breathing, certain her heart was going to explode, both from exertion and from all the emotions rushing through her. "I was thinking," she said. "If we went horseback riding all the time, we'd get nothing else done."

"I don't know," Chris said, stroking lazy fingers up and down her back. "I wouldn't call this nothing."

"No," she agreed, scooting closer so that she was spooned up against him. "I'll second that."

"I'm going to Australia in February," he said. "There's a place down there that's a combination spa and dude ranch."

The combination was so unusual she rolled over to look at him. "Massage on the trail? A facial peel from cow patties?"

"More high-end spa services and escorted trail rides for those who want the fresh air and exercise." He pushed a stray lock of hair out of her face. "You should come with me."

"Oh." Her breath hitched, but whether from his

words or his touch, she wasn't sure. She'd always wanted to see Australia. Had always wished that her dad would have done exactly what Chris was doing now. But she was no longer a kid without responsibilities, and bouncing off to satisfy a wanderlust was not the way to nail down partnership. "I couldn't."

"Why not?"

"Clients tend to get antsy when their attorneys disappear down under," she said. "Bosses, even more so."

"Do the words *vacation time* mean anything to you?"

"Not much," she admitted. She slid out of bed, then slipped on a robe. She moved to the wet bar, hoping she seemed casual, as if all she wanted was a drink, and not that she wanted to escape. "It's not that kind of job. Two weeks at Christmas is about as generous as any law firm on the planet gets, and I know the firm made the decision to shut down for those two weeks so that none of us would feel inclined to take a vacation the rest of the year."

"Did you go to law school or a prison camp?"

"Very funny."

She grabbed a diet soda from the mini fridge, then curled up on the couch.

"Now I've done it," he said. "I've managed to piss you off. I'm sorry."

She looked over at the bed. He did look sorry. He also looked incredibly sexy, and the truth was that she wanted to go with him to Australia more than she liked to admit. "It's a trade-off," she said. "I like my job. It's not as if I just picked it out of a hat and said, 'Hey, I think I'll be a lawyer today.' I actually like it. It means something to me." She liked the structure and the organization and the underlying fairness. As a kid, everything had seemed to happen without a reason. The house. The car. And maybe it was pop psychology, but she knew that was part of why she'd been attracted to the law, and to mediation in particular. Not just so that she'd have the paycheck, but so that she wouldn't be blindsided again. So that she'd have both understanding and control.

And that, she thought, was one of the reasons that she hated this whole partnership dance. She'd brought in seven solid clients over the course of the year. She'd billed an insane number of hours. And even so, she couldn't be sure she'd be offered partnership unless she landed one more client, all because her boss was hanging partnership over her head and the head of her office rival like a carrot. It infuriated her, but there was nothing she could do about it. She had no control, and the only thing that she could do to try to slide back in the drivers' seat was wrest the best damn client she could.

And that client was Russell Starr.

"There's e-mail and fax and global courier service," Chris said. "I manage to get a lot of work done when I travel." He got out of bed and came to sit next to her, his body, naked and glistening, making it hard for her to process his words.

"You work for yourself. I don't." She shrugged. "I've told you about my dad."

"That he barely managed to keep your family in food and shelter, yeah. You've mentioned it." He took her hand. "I like your dad. I've met him what, three times now? And he's a great guy, and I know you love him, but in that department, he gets a big, red F."

"Don't I know it," she said. "But that's my point. He was like you. He loved to travel and he would bounce all over the world at the drop of a hat, chasing a story."

"And that doesn't interest you."

"No, it does, actually. I always wished he would take me with him. I'd love to see the world. I'd love to go to the kinds of places you travel to."

"Then do it."

"See, that's what my dad would say."

"I already told you, I'm not your dad."

"I know," she said, though she could see the similarities between the two men and, yeah, it scared her. "I know you're not. But Chris, I'm not you, either. I can't just pick up and go. That's not who I am. It's not what I want."

"You want Russell Starr," he said, his expression hard.

She laughed. "Not like that. I swear. But as a client, yeah."

"And you like that? Scrambling to find a client because your boss said jump?"

She shrugged, trying for casual as she stood up. She needed to shower and go meet Russell. "Lawyers have to have clients. It's where the money comes from." But the truth was, she didn't like it. Not at all. Because he was right. This *was* about making the mice scramble for that damn piece of cheese.

And for the first time that she could remember, Alyssa wished she didn't want the morsel so damn much.

"YOU'RE TELLING ME Lorelei Leigh is in the hotel?" Alyssa said, referring to the former child superstar whose off-screen antics had turned her into a tabloid sensation. She knew the article about the resort had mentioned celebrities, but so far she hadn't seen one.

Beside Russell, Oliver Stanton sniffed. "The resort is host to a great number of well-known individuals," the resort manager said. "But most of them have not just punched their boyfriend in the face." He turned to look up at Russell. "This is going to turn into a publicity nightmare."

They were in Russell's private office on the top floor of the hotel, a Southwestern-style sanctuary that managed to be both austere and welcoming. The room was huge, with Russell's massive handcarved desk at one end and a conference table that would easily seat twenty at the other. At the moment, they were seated at the table, with Russell at the head and Oliver across from Alyssa.

Russell nodded briefly before turning his attention to Alyssa. "This is what I've been dealing with instead of riding the trails with you. Mark Crais—the boyfriend—filed charges for assault, and now Ms. Leigh's attorneys have told us they're filing a negligence action against the hotel claiming we shouldn't have allowed Mr. Crais on the premises."

"He's not a guest?"

"He's not."

"And they're trying to spin this into self-defense," Alyssa said. "This wasn't one of Lorelei Leigh's famous temper tantrums, it was her defending herself against a man the hotel should never have let onto the premises."

"Exactly."

"It's a nightmare," Oliver said again, his face pinched and his voice rising. "Opening weekend. The holidays. This is not the kind of publicity we need."

Russell's attention didn't stray from Alyssa. "I know you wanted to talk about legal representation, but I'm afraid right now I've got to deal with this. Can we talk when we get back to Dallas?"

Dallas, of course, would be too late. She needed him locked in before she returned to Texas. She needed to be able to swing by Kevin Prescott's house with a celebratory bottle of wine and the news that Starr Industries was in the pocket. But if Russell didn't want to talk, that goal had just shifted out of reach. Which meant she needed to make him talk now, and she needed to do it without being pushy.

What she needed, she realized, was to show him how useful having a firm like Prescott and Bayne on retainer could be.

"Dallas is fine, Russell," she said. "Obviously I'm not interested in inconveniencing you during a busy time. But before I go, do you mind if I make a suggestion?"

"Happy to hear it," he said.

"I've been developing a specialty as a mediator," she said, referring to the small practice she'd been building up offering her services as a go-between for parties who were trying to resolve their differences. "I still handle my own litigations, of course, but over the last three years, I've mediated dozens of cases. Kevin Prescott has been a great mentor in that regard, and he's been trying to really expand the firm to provide alternative dispute resolution services."

"And?" Oliver said, making Alyssa realize that she probably sounded a bit too much like a commercial.

"And I'm wondering if maybe we couldn't make all of this go away?"

"Go away?" Russell repeated. "You haven't talked to Ms. Leigh's assistant or her attorneys. I'm not sure that's possible."

"Maybe not," Alyssa admitted. "But you won't know until you try, and I'm happy to offer my services as mediator." She looked from Russell to Oliver and back to Russell again, and was pleased to see that both men looked interested. "My only condition is that if I'm able to bring the parties to a satisfactory conclusion, you give serious thought to retaining Prescott and Bayne. Starr Industries could save a lot of money annually if more disputes went to mediation, and by having the firm on retainer, we can advise you which matters are worth mediating and which are worth going to the mat for."

She held her breath and stood up straight, forcing herself to look calm and cool and not fidget with the buttons on her black silk suit. After a moment, Russell nodded. "Let me run it by my general counsel back in Dallas, but if he doesn't have an objection, neither do I. We'll have to get Leigh's and the boyfriend's attorneys into the mix, though, and I can't say whether they'll be interested."

"They have nothing to lose," Alyssa said. "If mediation doesn't go well, they just walk away and file their papers with the court."

"All right, then." He smiled, then held out his hand for her to shake. "I'll see if I can get it set up for tomorrow. I'll call you as soon as I know."

"Great." She nodded at both men, said her goodbyes and stepped from the office into the reception area.

"Do you need anything, Ms. Chambers?" Russell's secretary asked.

"Nope," Alyssa said. "I'm doing just fine."

MAX DALTON stared at the empty bed beside him. Never before had such a sight disturbed him. Usually it was he who urged the women to leave, gently but firmly pushing them out the door.

Today, though...

Today, he wanted nothing more than to have her back, and the truth was that he was jealous of the whole world. Because right then, the world had her, and he did not.

TWO HOURS in front of the computer and all Chris had to show for it were false starts and six sentences.

He glanced over at the mantel clock, willing time to

move faster. Willing her to return. Because without her by his side, he felt antsy.

No. That wasn't exactly true.

He felt antsy because she was with Russell. Having a business meeting. At least, he hoped it stayed all business, but considering the way Russell had looked at her when they'd met at the restaurant, and considering the conversation he'd overheard between her and Claire…

Except she'd told him there was no attraction there. That she'd dropped that ridiculous plan.

And the truth was, he believed her.

So why the hell was he in such a funk simply because she was off with Russell trying to do her job?

Because it's not about Russell. It's about men. It's about sex. It's about flings.

Yeah, well, true enough. Because the thought that he couldn't get out of his head was the very basic, very simple proposition that if she was willing to have a fling with him, then who else would she be willing to do the same with?

Maybe not at the same time—it's not like he thought she was downstairs having a wild time with the bartender—but next month. Next year.

Dammit.

He'd made a huge mistake agreeing to her terms. He'd been thinking with his dick, and his dick had wanted satisfaction. Chris wanted a life. A relationship. Chris wanted the whole damn picture.

A fling was only sex, and he wanted so much more than that.

But she'd made it clear in no uncertain terms that as far as a relationship was concerned, they were going nowhere fast. Relationship incompatible, which was really screwed up when you considered that they were completely compatible in every other aspect of their lives.

Frustrated, he snatched up the pen he'd been using to scribble notes and hurled it toward the door, almost knocking Alyssa in the head in the process as she burst inside, laughing and smiling.

"Holy cow!" she said. "What are you doing?"

"Scene not going well," he muttered, then scowled at her amused expression. "How come you're in such a good mood?"

"Because I am on my way to proving my worth to Starr Industries," she said.

"Meeting went well?"

"So far." She explained about the whole Lorelei Leigh thing, then ended with a shrug. "We'll see."

"Brilliant," he said, meaning it. "You really managed to twist that around to your advantage."

"Yeah, well, that's what I do. Shift people's perspectives. Negotiate deals. Convince side A to give a little and then convince side B to do the same so that the parties can come together satisfied."

"When you put it like that, it sounds awfully appealing." He slipped his hands around her waist and pressed a soft kiss to her mouth, thrilled when she took the casual kiss and turned it into something heated and wild. "Want to mediate me? I could use a little satisfaction."

She laughed, then glanced at the clock. "No time. I want to get my shopping done and get back before five so I don't miss the cutoff for shipping packages in time for Christmas. And I think I'd rather enjoy you slowly."

He couldn't argue with that. "Shopping for what?"

"I want to get one more thing for my parents," she said, then frowned at his computer. "But if your book is going badly, maybe I should just go alone."

"No, no," he lied as he watched her shimmy out of her suit skirt, then walk to the closet for her jeans. She slipped them on, looking up at him with a question in her eyes and not a smidgeon of self-consciousness. Less than twenty-four hours and they were already in a rhythm together. This wasn't a fling. No way was this a fling.

The only question was how he was going to convince Alyssa of what he already knew in his heart.

"Chris, you threw a pen at the door. I can shop by myself. And then we can do dinner or something. You're supposed to have time to work, remember?"

"The writing is going great," he lied. "You walked in on a tricky scene. Other than that, I've been exceptionally productive." He stood up and headed for his coat. "Besides, I need the local color for the article and today's blog post, so I'll still be working." How was that for justification? "So where are we going?"

As IT TURNED OUT, they weren't going far. Just a few miles north to the small town of Tesuque, more specifically to the Tesuque Glass Works.

"Isn't it fabulous?" Alyssa said as they walked into

the rustic wooden building decked out with eye-popping blue trim. Inside, the walls were adorned with stunning glass bowls and platters, all of which, they were told, were made on-site by master craftsmen.

"That's what you are," Alyssa said, taking his arm and easing up close. "A master craftsman, only you use a keyboard instead of blobs of molten glass."

"I hope I'm not one of those artistic masters who aren't discovered until after they're dead."

"Ha, ha." She bumped him with her hip. "Come check this out."

He moved to stand by her side, and they both looked through a glass panel into a viewing room and watched one of the craftsmen take a glob of red-hot glass, turn it on the end of a long pole and then shape it against a piece of metal.

"Hard to believe it starts out like that," she said. "All mushy and confused. And then it gets melded together into one of those." She turned and pointed to the exquisite bowls that decorated the showroom.

She rose up on her toes and brushed a kiss over his lips, then caught his lower lip between her teeth as she pulled away, leaving him with the very definite desire to do a little melding of his own. The trouble was, he wanted the melding to be more than physical. He wanted their lives fused together. And he wanted Alyssa to want that, too.

He shook it off, determined not to go there again. Just a few days ago he would have called a fool anyone who suggested he would have Alyssa in his bed. And now look where they were.

One step at a time, buddy. One step at a time.

He nodded toward the shelves. "So which one are you going to buy?"

"My mom loves blue," she said, picking out a large bowl with every shade of blue imaginable melted into the glass. "This would look gorgeous on their dining table, and she could put fruit or potpourri or something in it. What do you think?"

"She'll love it. What about your dad?"

"Still looking," she admitted. "I don't think glassworks is going to cut it."

"There's a silent auction in the lobby tonight," Chris said. "It was on the list of holiday events for tonight, along with cider and cookies and Santa for the kids, and a band and dancing for the grown-ups."

"Should we check it out?"

"Will you sit on Santa's lap?"

She lifted a brow. "You wouldn't be jealous?"

He laughed. "Good point. How about you just sit on my lap?"

She pressed a soft kiss to his lips. "Get me back to the hotel, and I'll do just that."

"Go," he said. "Pay. Hurry."

With a grin, she took the bowl to the counter, then waited while they wrapped it for shipping.

"So I was thinking about our analogy," she said, taking his hand as they walked back to the rental car. "The whole molten glass idea. And it seems to me that we ought to test it out."

"What do you mean?"

"The fusing part," she said, her mouth curving into a sultry smile. "I think maybe we ought to see just how much like glass we can be. You game?"

"Yeah," he said, the thought of a hot session of fusing with Alyssa enough to fuse his brain cells. "I am most definitely game."

11

"Wow," ALYSSA said, certain that she was going to melt, either from the heat of the shower or the heat the two of them had generated. "I think we came close to turning the water to steam."

"A little more practice, and we can hire ourselves out as a sauna," he said, just as relaxed and languid beside her.

"We should get out."

His hands skimmed over her. "Do we have to?"

She laughed, then pushed his hands away. "You're insatiable—"

"Only for you."

"—and we're supposed to be downstairs for the silent auction."

"All right," he said, reaching for a towel. "But I'm taking a rain check."

She got them both bottles of water from the minibar and that revived them somewhat, although Alyssa was certain the glow of sex had marked her. No worries. Once they saw Chris, they'd just be jealous.

She slipped a skirt on, then leaned back against the

dresser and watched him, still damp from the shower, as he dragged a comb through his hair then moved naked through the room. *He's mine,* she thought, then immediately closed her eyes and balled her hands into fists.

No. This wasn't heading for a permanent destination. They were firmly on the friendship-with-benefits plan. Any more, and she was risking everything. Her heart. Her security. Her entire vision of her future.

And she couldn't do that. She wouldn't let herself do that.

"You're not even dressed," he said, and she realized that her mind had wandered, and now he looked gorgeous in a knit shirt that hugged his fabulous chest and black jeans that showed off his perfect ass.

"Give me ten minutes," she said.

Actually, it took twelve, but when she pirouetted in front of him and saw the heat in his eyes, she decided the extra two minutes had been more than worth it.

They headed down together and found the lobby packed. There was a small orchestra in the corner, Santa's village near the Christmas tree, complete with an elf and a line of children, and waiters carrying trays of complimentary champagne and tasty appetizers. Around the edge of the room tables were set up, each displaying something fabulous and fun. A sheet of paper accompanied each item, and passersby placed escalating bids. When the auction wrapped up, the last—and highest—bidder won the item.

"This," she said, seeing a package for a three-night

stay at the resort. "I can get this for my dad, and then he can bring Mom. Perfect for a guy who likes to travel, right?" She scribbled her name and her bid, then realized that Chris was focused on the item next to her—a copy of *Life* magazine featuring Apollo 11 and signed by all the astronauts. "Wow. That's neat."

"And perfect for a guy with wanderlust," Chris said, then wrote his own name and bid. She peered over his shoulder and saw that the bidding was already up to $420.

"Chris! Are you crazy?"

"Not the last time I checked."

"I'm serious. That's a lot of money."

He sighed. "Alyssa, no matter what you might think, I'm capable of bringing in work, reasonably responsible and not even close to requiring public assistance."

"But—"

"I want the magazine."

And that, she thought, was the problem. Instead of saving, he just took what he wanted. *Crazy.* It drove her absolutely crazy.

"Quit worrying about me," he said, because he knew her far too well. "Come dance with me."

He didn't give her a chance to object, instead leading her to the dance floor and guiding her seamlessly around the floor. He was a perfect partner, and she had to admit that surprised her. She knew him well, but she didn't know everything. Not yet, anyway.

On their second turn around the floor, Russell caught her attention, and they stopped, moving to the side to join him. "I don't mean to interrupt," he said, "but I wanted to let you know we're all set for the mediation. Ten o'clock tomorrow. And thanks for doing this," he said to Alyssa. "I think it really may make the difference."

He moved away, and she turned to Chris who, she saw, was smiling.

"Sounds like you've got him wrapped up as a client."

"It's looking promising," she admitted.

"And then what happens?" He slipped his arm back around her waist and they glided back onto the floor.

She frowned, confused. "I make partner," she said. "It's what I've been working for."

"So do you have more freedom with partnership, or less? You said you wished you could travel, right? If you make partner will that happen?"

"Not right away," she admitted, feeling a bit miffed that he'd popped her partnership bubble. "It's an ownership interest, but it's not really your shop, so you still have to work your tail off and prove yourself."

"Then why not open your own shop?"

"What?"

"You like to travel and you can't. You don't like playing the political games that go along with law firms, but you put up with it. So why not open your own firm?" he asked. "Do what you're doing for Russell. Schedule mediations, have your secretary e-mail you the file. Prepare from Tuscany, and make sure you're in the office when the clients need you."

"You're living in fantasy land," she said, although in

truth the idea wasn't completely insane. She had a few friends who'd opened their own practices, and though she'd watched them struggle, after they were established, she'd envied them both their freedom and their incomes.

And if it meant that she could travel with Chris…

She shook it off. Travel was the least of their problems. He burned through money like it was going out of style. And although she wanted to see the world, she didn't want to live out of a suitcase, and two trips each month would pretty much kill her. And she wasn't the least bit interested in staying home while he traveled. Her mom had done that, and it was hell on her parents' relationship.

"It's an interesting idea," she finally admitted. "But not really practical."

He watched her for a moment, his expression unreadable. Then he nodded. "There's Santa. I'm pretty sure you promised to sit on his lap."

"I don't think so…"

"I want a picture," he said.

She protested, but not too hard. Why not sit on the big red guy's lap? Maybe he could tell her what she wanted for Christmas. Because right at the moment, Alyssa really didn't know.

THE MORNING SUN tickled Alyssa's nose, and she rolled over, reaching for Chris even in her sleep, only to find nothing but a cool spot on his side of the bed. She opened her eyes, then sat up stretching, her muscles sore from a long night with very little sleep and quite a bit of aerobic activity.

Not surprisingly, she found Chris parked at the desk, his headphones on, his fingers flying over the keys on his laptop. She sat at the edge of the bed, the sheet wrapped around her, and watched him work, his concentration impressing her as much as his creativity.

Part of her felt guilty—after all, if she hadn't come along, he'd have had each day, every day to work, and he probably would have finished the book by now, and made a lot more headway on the article.

But the guilt was short-lived and easily crushed. How could it not be? If she hadn't forced her way into his room, she never would have ended up in his bed.

Even that, though, held a tiny bit of regret. Because if she was honest with herself, she had to admit that she wanted more with him. More that she couldn't have, and so she needed to learn to be satisfied. To take what they'd promised each other, and to enjoy.

His fingers paused on the keys, and after a beat, he looked back over his shoulder. "Hey," he said. "How long have you been up?"

"Just a few minutes. I was watching you. It's cozy."

Something dark, almost sad, flashed in his eyes, but it was gone almost immediately, and she didn't call him on it. Instead, she got up and moved behind him, pressing her hands onto his shoulders. He felt tense, and she kneaded her fingers into his skin, wanting him loose and at ease. After a moment of that, though, he shrugged out from under her.

"Chris?"

"Sorry. Just lost in my characters." He spoke without meeting her eyes, and though his words were perfectly reasonable, she couldn't shake the feeling that he was lying.

"Well, that's good," she said brightly. "Because you have all day with them. I've got the mediation this morning, and that will probably take hours. And then I need to run a few errands." Specifically, she needed to find him a present. It was Tuesday, and Christmas was in two days. And though she'd looked around—in Santa Fe, at the silent auction, in the glass works— she'd found nothing special enough to get him.

"I'll miss you," he said, managing to make three little words as provocative as a phone sex come-on.

"No, you won't," she said, teasing, and telling herself that they did not have time for a quickie, not if she wanted to make a good impression, arrive early, and review the summaries that Russell had asked the attorneys to put together for her.

"Every minute," he said sincerely. "But I'll muddle through."

"Glad to hear it." She kissed him, hard and hot and with as much promise as she could put into it, and when she pulled away the heat she saw in his eyes made her tingle with feminine satisfaction. "Previews of coming attractions," she said, then laughed as he made a grab for her. "No, no, no," she said. "Not until we both get some work done."

"You're an evil vixen," he said.

She blew him a kiss as she danced toward the bathroom. "Don't you forget it."

While he worked, she took a shower, got dressed and downed a cup of coffee from the tray he'd ordered from room service.

"You're a god among men," she said.

"Tell me something I don't know."

"And cinnamon rolls," she said, looking at the four rolls on a Christmas-tree-shaped plate. "That part makes you a devil. Do you know what that will do to my hips?"

"Your hips are perfect."

"Yeah?" She checked the clock, realized she'd gotten ready in record time, and rethought her whole getting-early-to-the-job plan. "You want to do a quality-control inspection on my hips?" she asked, reaching back to unzip her skirt.

"I think I'm familiar with their quality," he said.

"Oh." She zipped herself back up. "Right."

His shoulders sagged. "Sorry. The story's kicking my ass, and I need to spend a chunk of today wandering the resort and talking to the staff and the guests, so I lose that time to work on it."

"And I'm distracting you. Exactly like I was afraid I would."

"No," he said, getting up to get coffee. "It's okay. It's not that."

"Not *that?*" she repeated. "But there is something the matter. What is it?"

"Nothing, Alyssa. It's nothing."

"The hell it is."

He ran his hands through his hair, then sighed audibly, his expression shifting from irritated to apologetic. "Shit, I'm sorry. I'm being an ass. Go. Go forth and acquire much legal business, and by the time you get back I'll have beaten this book into submission and will no longer be a prick. I swear."

"That's really all it is?"

"Promise," he said.

"Okay." She squeezed his hand, then eased in for a kiss, catching him on the side of his mouth.

"Sorry. Cinnamon roll," he said, but as she slid out the door to go meet Russell, she couldn't escape the sinking feeling in her stomach that there was something wrong that went deeper than either characters or confections.

CHRIS STARED at the words on his computer screen and sighed. He'd written a dozen pages already, the words flying out.

Which was a good thing.

Too bad the words weren't following the outline of the book he'd turned in.

Max Dalton was in love. And the superspy was frustrated as hell that the sentiment wasn't returned.

Gee. Wonder where that came from?

He stood up and poured himself a fresh cup of coffee. In truth, he was certain that Alyssa *did* love him. But he was equally certain that she wasn't going to do a damn thing about it.

Worse, he had to tell her how he felt, and as much as he would miss the press of her body against his, he had to shut down this arrangement they'd created. Because it drove him crazy. Knowing he could touch her so intimately without any real intimacy at all. Friendship, sure. But he wanted more.

He wanted it all.

And he didn't know how to convince her that they could have it.

"I'M AMAZED, but I think we're actually making progress," Russell said, drawing Alyssa into the small conference room they'd set up as her makeshift office. Each of the other parties—Lorelei Leigh's entourage, Mike Crais's group of friends and attorneys, and the Starr resort management—had a similar room they called home base, and they'd been spending the last five hours coming back and forth into Alyssa's room, as she tried various approaches to get them to reach a happy medium.

"It's a win-win," Alyssa said, referring to the most recent plan they'd hammered out. All charges would be dropped, no new charges would be filed, and Lorelei and Mike would act as the celebrity auctioneers at the Christmas Eve fundraising auction that was going to wrap up the next night's party. The suggestion had been a long shot in light of the acrimony between the two. But at the same time, Alyssa knew she was dealing with celebrities, to whom image meant everything. And what better way to divert attention from an unpleasant punch in the face than to wrap it up in a bow and drown it in Christmas cheer? And undoubtedly gain some last-minute publicity for the Starr Resort fundraiser.

"You said you do a lot of this kind of thing?"

"Not too many celebrities in Dallas," Alyssa said, peering at the screen on her laptop and reviewing the language of the agreement she'd drafted for the parties to sign. "But a good deal of my practice is mediation, yes."

"You're good at it," he said.

"Yes," she said, looking up and giving him a smile. "I am." She drew in a breath, figuring it was now or never. "Prescott and Bayne has a lot of talented people, Russell, and we'd like to be part of your team."

"So I gathered," he said as a quick knock sounded at the door, followed by Oliver Stanton's flushed face.

"I can't believe it, but I think we managed it. And in time for us to get a blurb on the local news, too."

"That's great," Russell said, and Alyssa heartily seconded the sentiment.

"Tell them to hang tight and I'll have an agreement to them in the next five minutes."

"We should celebrate," Russell said. "The closing of this deal, and the fact that Starr Industries has found a stellar new law firm to retain."

Her heart did a little back-flip number. "Seriously?"

"I don't joke where business is concerned. Congratulations, Alyssa. You always were the smart girl in school. I know I'm putting my business in good hands." He held out his hand to shake, and she took it, trying to stay calm and professional when all she wanted to do was run around the room screaming with glee.

"I've got to do a bit of publicity with Ms. Leigh and Mr. Crais, but can I buy you a drink? I know a local resort with a fabulous bar."

She laughed. "Any other time and I'd say yes," she said, "but I have last-minute shopping to do." She had to find a gift for Chris, and the stores were going to close in just a couple of hours. Not to mention the fact that she was dying to share her good news. She'd hold off, though, and let him write. Then she'd jump him and celebrate in style. Naked room-service champagne sounded appealing.

"Alyssa?"

"Sorry. Mind wandering." She hoped she wasn't blushing. "Let's get this agreement signed. And then maybe you can point me to some of the cooler shops in town."

"I can try," he said. "What do you have in mind?"

It turned out that Russell did more than try. He told her exactly which store to go to for what she had in mind, and after only forty-five minutes, Alyssa had not only bought a dozen ornaments for which she had no tree, but she'd found Chris's perfect present, exactly in the store that Russell had suggested.

Now she was trying to balance the huge box she'd hidden in a green trash bag and manage to open the hotel-room door at the same time. Not an easy trick, and she was still working the card key when the knob turned, the door pulled open and Chris was standing there, looking like a man whose day had not been anywhere near as perfect as hers.

"You okay?" she asked, sliding the bag with the box onto the dining table.

"Fine," he said, sitting back down at the computer, his fingers once again poised over the keys.

O-kay.

No, she amended, *not okay.*

Something was bugging him, and before they'd signed up for their fling arrangement, he'd always griped to her. Usually over a glass of wine and a backdrop of bad television. If sex was the reason he was being so close-mouthed now, then that was completely and totally unacceptable. They'd made an agreement, after all. The fling was not supposed to impact their friendship.

"Hey," she said, going over and putting her hands on his chair back. "What's wrong?"

His shoulders rose and fell as he drew in a breath. For a moment, she thought he was going to say something, then he closed his mouth.

"Chris?"

"It's nothing."

"Oh, yeah. Like I'm going to believe that."

He turned to face her. "The book," he said. "It's just the book."

She licked her lips, not believing him, but not having the slightest clue what the real problem could be.

"Okay," she said, sitting on the edge of the bed. "Pages coming slowly?"

"Actually, I seem to be spitting out pages at a phenomenal rate."

"So what's not working right?" she asked.

He stared at her, the moment so long it almost became uncomfortable.

"The characters," he finally said. "They're not behaving the way I was expecting them to. The way I wanted them to."

"Oh. Well, I'm not a writer, but since you're the author, can't you just, I don't know, *fix* it?"

"I wish I could."

She stood up, weirdly uncomfortable. "Well, maybe if you tell me what's going on."

"Max, for one thing. He's completely besotted with Natalia."

"I think that's sweet."

"He's not supposed to be a man who gets tied into knots because of a woman."

"Maybe he's changing?"

"Yeah," he said, running his fingers through his hair. "I think he is. And you know what? That would be fine. Except he's about to crash and burn in a big way."

"Because of Natalia?"

"I have this vision of them together, you know? Fighting the bad guys. Blowing shit up. A team. Nick and Nora with bombs and guns."

"I think that sounds awesome," she said, thinking about the first Dalton book that she'd read as a pile of printed pages. She'd loved it, but how much more fun if Dalton had a female counterpart to spar with?

"Would be," he agreed. "Except Natalia isn't interested in getting tied down with Max. She's got her own operation, and she likes it that way."

"Well, like I said. You're the author. Can't you fix it?"

He glanced at her face. "It's not always that easy."

"Oh." She shifted on the bed, unable to shake the feeling that he wasn't telling her everything. "I, um, wish I could help."

He looked at her then, hard and steady. "Yeah. I wish you could, too."

She exhaled, because this was too much. "Dammit, Chris. What's really bugging you?"

"The book. I told you."

"No," she said, then sighed. "You swore things wouldn't change if we slept together, and now look at us. You used to tell me what was on your mind. Dammit, Chris, you're my best friend."

"Friend," he said, sounding so completely sad that it broke her heart. This was not good. This was so, so, so not good, and she didn't know how to fix it because she didn't know what was wrong.

"Chris, please."

He ran his fingers through his hair. "I've been working all day," he said. "I'm going to go take a shower."

She tamped down the urge to insist again, and tried changing tack. "Want some company?"

"Thanks, but I think I'll take this one solo."

He slipped into the bathroom, and she leaned

forward, her head buried in her hands, her relief disappearing as fast as it had come. Something had set him off, and she didn't know what. How was she supposed to make it better if she didn't know what the problem was? If he wouldn't even talk to her?

She pondered the problem as she lugged the green bag to the closet, then hid it beneath her suitcase. That errand accomplished, she eyed the bathroom door, then went over and put her hand on the knob. He'd said he wanted to be alone, but she needed him. Needed to feel close to him again. Because some sort of wall had been built between them, and it was terrifying her. At least she'd lost Bob after a relationship. She wasn't about to lose Chris after only a few days.

She had to go in.

Except she couldn't. He'd locked the damn door.

Frustrated, she paced the room, then paused in front of the computer. He'd said the book was what was giving him grief, so maybe…

She peered down at the scene he was working on. Natalia, trapped in the bad guy's lair, naked and bound to the wall. And Max coming in, not certain she'd really been captured, but fearing it was a trap and that she was working with the enemy.

Max knew he should call her on it. Knew he should back away. Run away.

Except he wanted her. Wanted her so badly that it was worth the danger.

And as Alyssa read the pages—as Max Dalton took the bound-in-chains Natalia, claiming her body as his own even though he feared that she'd switched allegiance to the villain—she felt her own body warm, felt her sex tingle.

The pages were hot. Burn-the-computer-up hot.

More than that, though, the pages gave her a delicious, decadent, fabulous idea.

And with that thought, Alyssa crossed to the bed and smiled.

CHRIS STOOD in the shower, letting the hot water pound over him. Sting his skin. Punish him for being such a total ass.

She was right, of course. He needed to talk to her. Needed to cut short their fling and backtrack to just friends.

Easier said than done, though. Because he knew damn well that they'd never be "just friends" again. Not really. Not after this.

Worse, he didn't want to be just her friend. He wanted all of her, and it ate at him, deep in his gut, to know that he couldn't have her.

You don't know that for sure.

He shook his head, because technically that was true. He didn't know.

Practically, he knew damn well that she'd kick him to the curb if he suggested anything permanent between them.

He had to try, though. Had to put the brakes on their fling, sit her down for a talk and, he thought hopefully, they could start back up again as a solid, legitimate couple.

He tilted his head back and let the spray pound his face. A guy could dream, couldn't he?

Determined, he turned the water off, then toweled himself dry. Still damp, he wrapped a towel around his waist, then navigated through the steam-filled bathroom to the door. He pulled open the door, stepped into the room and gasped.

"Hey," Alyssa said from where she lay naked in bed. "I thought you might want me to help a little with that scene you were stuck on."

He swallowed, his entire body going hard as stone. Because she wasn't just in bed. She wasn't just naked.

Somehow she'd managed to bind both her wrists to the bars of the headboard with the sashes from their two hotel robes.

"Uh, how did you—"

"Slip knots," she said, a sensual gleam in her eye. "You gonna come set me free?"

Not in this lifetime. He moved to the foot of the bed, his plan to break off their fling flying right out the window. He was a man, after all, not a saint. And dear God, he wanted one last taste of heaven. "I think I'll leave you just the way you are."

"Good," she said, then grinned. "I think we have just enough time for some in-depth research before dinner."

He dropped the towel, then eased onto the bed. "This isn't going to be slow and easy," he said, because his body was tight, desperate with the need to claim her. To mark her and keep her.

A corner of her mouth lifted. "Prove it."

He accepted the challenge, spreading her legs, then sliding his fingers over her center, his body going even harder when he found her wet and ready for him.

"Don't wait," she said. "I need you. I need you inside me."

It was an invitation he wouldn't dream of declining, and he slipped on a condom, then eased over her. He thrust deep inside, losing himself to the glorious sensation of being connected with her again, of being back in rhythm with her.

She arched up, meeting him, her arms still bound so that he had total control. A control he shamelessly took advantage of, teasing her with his thrusts, slow and easy, then hard and fast, until she was begging him and he was desperate for release.

They came together, and he collapsed, gasping, by her side, his fingers stroking her bare skin, his eyes on her face.

This was, he realized, exactly what he needed. A symbol that she was his. And that no matter what happened, she always would be.

He stroked her cheek, wishing they could stay like this forever, and at the same time not wanting to be stagnant. For better or for worse, he wanted a change of agenda with Alyssa. He only hoped that in the end, it would be for better.

He released her arms, then pulled her close. She snuggled up against him, then sighed contentedly and closed her eyes.

"Alyssa?" he said, but he got no response. She was

fast asleep, and a moment later, he joined her, enjoying the feel of her naked body next to his, and fearing that tonight might be the last night that he experienced such heaven.

MORNING CAME only seconds after he drifted off, or at least it felt that way, and he woke to see her smiling at him.

"Merry Christmas Eve," he said.

"I have good news. I meant to tell you last night."

"Russell," he said, feeling like a heel. "I should have asked."

"Considering I went out of my way to distract you, you're forgiven. But I got it." She hugged him close. "I can't believe I got it!"

"How could he not want to hire you? You're brilliant. And Prescott and Bayne would be insane not to offer you partnership after that." He knew the job would keep her even more tied down than she already was, but he also knew she wanted it, and so he was happy for her. Truly he was.

At the same time—

"Alyssa."

She'd been telling him about the mediation, but now she stopped, looking up at him with a question in her eyes.

"I'm sorry," he said. "I know my timing stinks, but I can't—I just can't do this any longer."

She shifted, easing away from him, her expression wary. "Do what?"

"The fling," he said. "Alyssa, I'm sorry. I have to break our contract."

12

His words hit her like a slap across the face, and she scrambled backwards until she was pressed against the headboard, her hands clutching the sheet to her chest.

"No," he said, his expression mortified. "Not you. *This.*" He gestured between them. "I don't want this. I don't want a fling."

She licked her lips and eyed him, not sure how to respond because the world had just shifted, and he was the one who'd pulled the rug out from under her. "You sure seemed to want it last night when you were inside me."

He flinched, and she immediately regretted the crudity. But dammit, he'd *hurt* her.

"I want *you,* Alyssa. Not a fling. Not just a friendship. I want *you.*" He drew in a deep breath and looked helplessly at her. "I want all of you."

For a moment—one brief, shining moment—his words flooded her heart, filling her with a sweet kind of joy.

Then the bubble burst and the real world came crashing down on her shoulders. She grabbed a pillow and tossed it at him. "Dammit, Chris. Damn *you*."

She slid out of the bed and stormed to the bathroom where she'd left her jeans and sweatshirt the day before. How could she have been so stupid? She'd told herself not to have a fling with him. Told herself it would end badly, and now—big surprise—that's exactly where they were.

Dammit, dammit, dammit.

"Alyssa, please. Listen."

She rounded on him, naked, her clothes in her hand. "No, *you* listen. We had a deal. We made an agreement. A contract. And you have just blown it."

"I have," he agreed. "But I want a different agreement. I want a different contract. Dammit, Alyssa. I want you. All of you. And I want you forever."

She could feel the tears streaming down her face and didn't bother to brush them away. "You think I don't want *you?*" she asked. "I do. And that's why we had our agreement, remember? So we can have each other. Friendship. Sex. It's perfect." Even as she said it, the words felt cold. But cold didn't mean wrong, and she'd thought this through enough to know that she was right.

"And what happens when one of us meets somebody?" he asked, and she forced herself not to flinch in horror at the thought of him making love to another woman. "What happens to our arrangement then?"

"We stop," she said, her heart twisting.

He shook his head. "We stop now. Stop," he repeated, "and start up again different. Better."

"I told you, Chris. I *told* you. I can't do this with you. We have nowhere to go."

"We have everywhere to go," he said, taking her hands. "Come with me. Come to Australia. Come to Paris. You want to travel, Alyssa. Travel with me."

"Are you seriously insane? I'm an attorney, in case you forgot. You want me so badly, then maybe you should be the one who shifts gears. Get a regular job. Buy some freaking car insurance and a car to go with it. Because I can't live hand to mouth, Chris. I won't. And I won't sit back and watch while the man I love does that, either."

"You love me," he said, his words so soft they made her want to melt.

"You know I do," she said, wishing desperately that made a difference.

"Then why can't you meet me halfway?"

"Sounds to me like I'm the only one doing the moving," she said.

"What do you want? Do you want to hear me say I have a retirement account? I do. Two, actually. My old one from my days as a stringer, and a new one that I put ten percent of every check into."

She cocked her head, looking at him. "You're telling me that you actually have money in the bank for when you retire?"

"Well, not a million dollars, but it's growing."

"And you save. Whenever money comes in?"

"Yes, I do." He moved forward and took her hands. "But that's not the point. I want us together because we're good together. Not because of retirement accounts and paychecks."

"Retirement accounts and paychecks are what make the world go round, Chris. And if you don't know that, then we're too far apart ever to find a middle ground." She pressed her lips together, wishing it weren't true, but knowing it was. "Dammit," she said, then kicked her foot, trying to get through the bunched-up clump of denim. "I have to go out. I have to walk around."

"Alyssa. No." He reached out, then grabbed her elbow as she was trying to slide her shirt on.

She sagged. "Don't you see, Chris? We had it perfect. You couldn't have let it stay perfect at least through Christmas?"

"I was hoping to make it better," he said, the lines on his face hard. Maybe she wasn't playing fair, but he'd started it, and she told herself she felt no guilt.

More than that, she told herself she wasn't tempted by what he was offering. Because she knew better than to think it was real. Sweet words and a nice life, but in the harsh light of reality, she'd be faced with the kind of life she'd sworn she would never live. Her mom and dad loved, and deeply, but their day-to-day life had been a living hell at times. And to Alyssa's mind, even love couldn't conquer all.

THE HOTEL ROOM seemed smaller now that Alyssa had gone, as if she'd taken every bit of sparkle and hope with her.

Not a bad description, Chris thought. On a normal day, he'd write the words down, planning to use them later in one of his books.

Today, however, wasn't normal.

He'd hurt her, and the knowledge that he'd done that twisted in his gut like a living thing.

He hadn't had a choice, though. He wanted the woman too much to continue the fantasy. And though he couldn't regret what he'd done, he damn sure regretted the result, and he cursed Alyssa and all her damn hang-ups about money.

At the same time, though…

Well, at the same time he had to admit that maybe she'd been right. Maybe the scenario he'd laid out only asked her to change, while he kept on his merry way.

It was idiotic, of course, because he could manage his life just fine, thank you very much. Except that the way he managed it mattered to Alyssa. Mattered a lot.

And she mattered to him.

So he needed to make some hard decisions. Like, which was more important—glomming his free time to write and bouncing all over the globe when it suited him, or the woman he loved.

He drew in a breath.

Honestly, it wasn't that hard a decision after all. Because in the end, for him, Alyssa would always win.

The question was, what to do now?

He was willing to make some sacrifices, sure. But a regular, nine-to-five work schedule wasn't on the agenda. He liked having time to work on his book, and until he sold or Lil told him to forget about it, that was a dream he intended to pursue.

As for travel, he'd cut back, but he wasn't about to give it up entirely. For one thing, he was already established as a travel writer, and the thought of shifting his freelance career to another focus gave him hives. Bottom line, though, was that he loved it. Loved exploring new places and visiting old favorites.

And he would love it even more with Alyssa at his side.

She could do it, too. All she had to do was think creatively and give a little. But he knew Alyssa, and despite her soft curves, she could be damn rigid. And about this, he feared she was going to be unbendable steel.

Steel, however, wouldn't work. They'd both have to bend a little if they were going to come together on this.

And despite the fact that she'd walked out, he still held out hope. She'd said she loved him, and he knew it was true. Knew it well enough that he intended to go out and find her.

And when he did, he only hoped she'd be willing to negotiate her own life the way she negotiated for her clients, searching for a middle ground that everyone could live with. More than that, he hoped that she wanted him enough—*loved* him enough—to make the effort.

"Alyssa?"

Alyssa looked up into Russell's concerned face.

"Are you okay?"

She was sitting on a bench near the valet stand, huddled into her coat. The valet had asked for her ticket, and then given her the strangest look when she'd said she didn't have one, and had proceeded to sit. Apparently, he'd called upstairs about the crazy lady at the entrance early in the morning on Christmas Eve.

"I'm fine. I just—oh, hell. Chris and I had a fight."

He nodded, then extended his arm. "Let me buy you a drink."

She hesitated, then took it, following him into the elevator before she thought to ask where they were going.

"My office," he said. "You looked like you could use a friend, and I happen to be available. I also happen to have a full bar in my office, so whatever you want, I've got."

"How are you at relationships?" she asked.

"Considering I seem to start a new one every six or so weeks, I'd have to say pretty lousy."

She laughed. Couldn't argue with that.

"But I'm great at advice," he said, ushering her in. "Comes with the job. I have an opinion on everything."

She almost poured her heart out to him, but stopped herself. This wasn't something she wanted input on. She needed to look inside her own heart and figure out what she wanted to do. She told Russell as much. "And then I need to sit down with Chris and figure out where we are."

"Fair enough," Russell said. He passed her a vodka tonic. "So what are you going to do now? Head back to your room?"

She rubbed the leather and silver bracelet she'd been wearing since Sunday. "No. I need to think first. Figure out what I want. What's non-negotiable. And hopefully find a lot of places where we can intersect." She looked up at him. "You don't have any spare rooms, do you?"

He reached into his desk and pulled out a key. "My personal suite. It's yours for the day."

"I couldn't—"

"You can," he said. "And you will. It's empty. I'll be here working on the party for tonight. You're still coming?"

She nodded. "I hope not alone."

"Good luck. If Chris comes knocking, should I send him to you?"

For a moment, she considered saying yes. But she shook her head no. She needed time alone. "Just tell him you don't know." She paused in the doorway. "Russell, can I ask you a question?"

"Of course."

"Are you hiring Prescott and Bayne? Or are you hiring me?"

Russell's smile was all business and all-knowing. "You're the one who impressed me, Alyssa. I'm hiring you."

THE BALLROOM was stunning. The band spectacular. The appetizers exceptional.

Chris really didn't care.

He'd waited all day for Alyssa, and she hadn't

returned. He wasn't even going to go down to the damn party, but he was afraid that if he didn't, she would and he'd miss her.

Considering the crowd, though, she could be standing five feet away and he'd still miss her.

Dammit, he just wanted her beside him. Wanted to talk to her. Wanted to know that she was safe.

Not that he was really worried, but he'd tried her cell phone, only to have it ring in the hotel room with him. And when he'd called the concierge, the man had been eager to please but uninformed.

Honestly, if he didn't find her tonight, he was calling out the dogs.

All around the room, people were mingling and laughing. Couples were standing just a little too close. Kids were playing chase around the Christmas tree. Even Lorelei Leigh and Mark Crais were holding court amid a cluster of reporters anxious for a post-auction interview.

Alyssa, however, was nowhere to be found.

Chris glanced at his watch and saw that it was already after ten. He grabbed a glass of champagne from a passing waiter, hating this feeling of helplessness. He wanted her. So why wasn't she there? Why wasn't she in his arms where she belonged? And what the hell could he do to get her there?

He didn't have an answer to that question, and since his tolerance for holiday cheer was beginning to ebb, he stepped out of the ballroom and onto the patio, which was warm despite the dropping temperature because of the outdoor heaters. The fire from above glowed down, casting the night in orange light. It was, he thought, a romantic picture, and he wished Alyssa were there to share it with him.

She wasn't, though, and he turned to head back to his room.

That's when he saw her, looking so beautiful he was sure the crowd would part for her like the Red Sea. She'd clearly gone back to the room, as he recognized the dress, and he wondered if she'd gone to change clothes or to look for him.

From the way her eyes were skimming the crowd, he assumed the latter, and his heart leapt a little as hope flared.

"Here," he whispered. And though there was no way she could have heard him, she looked up, she saw him, and she smiled.

He moved forward, then opened the door for her, not even bothering for nonchalant. "Alyssa."

She held up a hand, and he feared that he'd blown it. That it was too late, and she was only coming to say goodbye.

"I wrote a mediation statement," she said, and of all the things in the world he could have expected her to say, that really wasn't on the list.

"You what?"

"I want it to work," she said, lifting her chin and tossing her shoulders back. She was wearing a red gown with a strap over only one shoulder, and in that posture she looked so unbelievably sexy that he almost couldn't keep his hands off her.

And he said a silent prayer that he wouldn't have to keep them off much longer.

She pulled a sheet of paper from her evening bag. "So I did what I require my clients to do. Wrote down what's non-negotiable, and then listed everything else."

"All right," he said, nodding. "What's non-negotiable?"

She licked her lips, then looked up at him. "You."

The word caught him like a punch to the stomach. "What?" He feared he was misunderstanding. That she was telling him to go, not stay.

"You," she repeated, her voice so soft it told him everything he wanted to know. She wanted him, and he thought his body would collapse with relief.

"Don't mistake me," she continued. "I have a lot of other issues, but the point is that I'm willing to compromise on them. But I know what I need to make this a successful mediation, and that's to walk back to the room with you."

He couldn't stop the grin that spread wide. "That's my bottom line, too."

"Then I think we're going to make this work," she said. "I think we can, if we both give a little."

He stroked her cheek. "I love you, Alyssa. And if it's important to you, I'll even find a regular job."

Her brows lifted. "You'd do that?"

"We're negotiating, right? Didn't you once tell me that's the way it works? Each side gives a little? Well, I can't stomach the nine-to-five thing, but I'm pretty sure I can find a job teaching as an adjunct, and that should not only have flexible hours, but allow me a lot of time to travel." He cocked his head. "And that probably brings us to our first point of contention. Because you don't want me going away, and I want you to go with me."

"Okay," she said, her eyes teasing.

"Come again?"

"I said okay. I'll travel with you." She held up a finger. "Not the insane schedule you have now because, hey, I like hanging out at home. But I want to be with you, and I want to travel."

"And I want you to. But what about your job? That speech about how you don't have time."

"Well," she said, looking both proud and sheepish, "I'm working on that. But I think you may have had the right idea. I spent the day making phone calls to clients and colleagues and I'm thinking I may open my own firm."

"And the boss can travel when she wants."

"So long as she has a phone with e-mail and the travel doesn't screw with her clients, then, yeah. She sure can."

She stepped closer and eased her arms around his neck. "What do you think? Can we find a happy medium?"

Chris was pretty sure his heart was going to explode. "I'm going with an enthusiastic yes."

She tilted her face up to him in silent invitation, and he accepted without hesitation. It had only been hours, but he'd missed the feel of her, the taste of her. And damned if he didn't want more. Right then.

"Let's get out of here," he said.

"Good idea," she murmured, sighing in his arms.

He held out his elbow for her to take. "What about money? You aren't going to grill me on that?"

She licked her lips. "I've decided that's an area that I can back off on. After all, I make good money. And like you said, you're not destitute."

"Alyssa," he said. "I'm proud of you."

They managed to get to the door before the final question came, just as he'd suspected it would.

"But you were telling me the truth about having a retirement plan, right?"

"Yeah," he assured her. "I was."

ALYSSA WASN'T SURE when she'd felt more free or more terrified. She was about to go out into the professional world and jump without a net. That was the scary part.

The part that kept her sane? That Chris would be there to catch her.

They slipped inside the hotel room and his fingers went immediately to her zipper.

She laughed, then slid away from him. "Hold that thought," she said. "I've got something for you. I wanted to give it to you earlier, but we decided to have our first fight instead."

"I thought we ought to get it out of the way," he said, deadpan. "You know. Make it easier to move on with the rest of our lives."

"Very thoughtful," she said, from where she was rummaging in the closet.

She returned with a large box, and when she plopped it on the bed, the mattress sagged under the weight of the thing.

"What on earth?"

"Open it," she said. "Go on."

He didn't argue, just peeled back the paper to reveal a large box that at one point had held hotel-quality linens. He opened the box, pulled out the packing and gasped in awe. "Alyssa. It's…perfect."

Yes, she thought, it was. An antique Remington typewriter restored to shining perfection. Gently he lifted it out of the box, then found a piece of hotel stationery and fed it into the machine. He tapped a letter and the machine responded perfectly.

"I found it in town. I wanted to surprise you."

"It's wonderful," he said, squeezing her hand. "You're wonderful."

He finished typing, then stepped aside, letting her see what he'd written.

I LOVE YOU.

"Come here," she said, drawing him into her arms, "and show me."

He pulled her close, then kissed her hard, and she pressed close, wanting to feel every inch of him, wanting to know that this was real.

On the mantel, the clock struck midnight.

"Merry Christmas," she said.

"You're all I ever wanted," he said.

"You have me."

He brushed a kiss across her lips. "Then this one's

going down in the record books as the best Christmas ever."

"Yeah," she said, snuggling close. "It most certainly is."

Epilogue

"No," ALYSSA said into her cell phone as the plane sat on the tarmac, "I can't schedule another mediation on the fourteenth if there's one already set for the morning. I don't care if we expect it to be short, I always antici-pate them running long." She paused, then held up a finger to Chris to let him know she'd only be another minute. "I'll be back in two weeks. Just work it out, okay? And schedule an appointment with Russell Starr for the week after I get back. Right. Thanks. We're going to take off soon, so I should go. Bye."

She clicked off, then looked at Chris. "Insanity."

"Nervous?"

"About flying? You know it. I still think we should make out the entire way. How nervous can I be if we're having a wild make-out session?"

"I'm pretty sure the airline frowns on that. But I was actually talking about this week. First time away since you've stepped out on your own. Scared?"

"Terrified."

"You have a great staff and you're well-connected," he added, tapping the phone. "It's going to be fine."

"I know it is." She squeezed his hand. "And I wouldn't miss this trip for the world." As she'd once told him, she'd always wanted to see Australia, and now they were going together, him for his article and her to sightsee and be a sloth. Sounded like heaven, actually.

He leaned in and pressed a kiss to her lips. It started soft, then heated up, just the way it always did with Chris.

Always did, Alyssa thought. *And always would.*

"If you get nervous," he said, "just hold my hand."

"I'll do that anyway," she said, taking it, then exhaling a little gasp when something hard poked her palm. "What the—"

She opened her hand and turned it over, revealing a solitaire diamond sparkling in a platinum setting. "Chris. Oh, my God. This is—" She met his eyes. "This is too much."

"Not for a man who just sold the first three books in the Max Dalton series." He grinned widely as she worked to hold back her squeal.

She couldn't help it, though, and she flung her arms around him. "That's amazing! Congratulations!"

"Lil called this morning."

"That's fabulous, but you still didn't have to buy—"

"Yeah," he said firmly. "I did." He unstrapped his belt, then moved into the aisle and bent down onto one knee. "Alyssa Chambers, you've been my best friend for years. Now I'm asking you to be my wife."

"Yes," she whispered as the passengers in the seats surrounding them burst into applause. And as he slipped the ring onto her finger, Alyssa thought back to a chilly night in a carriage in Dallas last Christmas season. She'd wanted romance that night, and it was still hard to believe that she'd found a lifetime supply of it.

And it was even harder to believe that her perfect man had been right under her nose the whole time.

'THIS EVENING I'm flying to New York for two weeks,'
Jasim imparted with a casualness that made her heart sink
like a stone. 'That's why I had you brought here. I own this
apartment and you'll be comfortable here while I'm abroad.'

'I can afford my own accommodation although I may not
need it for long. I'll have another job by the time you
get back—'

Jasim released a slightly harsh laugh. 'There's no need for
you to look for another position. How would I ever see you?
Don't you understand what I'm offering you?'

Elinor stood very still. 'No, I must be incredibly thick
because I haven't quite worked out yet what you're offering
me....'

His charismatic smile slashed his lean dark visage.
'Naturally, I want to take care of you....'

HPEX0110A

'No, thanks.' Elinor forced a smile and mentally willed him not to demean her with some sordid proposition. 'The only man who will ever take *care* of me with my agreement will be my husband. I'm willing to wait for you to come back but I'm not willing to be kept by you. I'm a very independent woman and what I give, I give freely.'

Jasim frowned. 'You make it all sound so serious.'

'What happened between us last night left pure chaos in its wake. Right now, I don't know whether I'm on my head or my heels. I'll stay for a while because I have nowhere else to go in the short term. So maybe it's good that you'll be away for a while.'

Jasim pulled out his wallet to extract a card. 'My private number,' he told her, presenting her with it as though it was a precious gift, which indeed it was. Many women would have done just about anything to gain access to that direct hotline to him, but his staff guarded his privacy with scrupulous care.

Before he could close the wallet, his blood ran cold in his veins. How could he have made such a serious oversight? What if he had got her pregnant? He knew that an unplanned pregnancy would engulf his life like an avalanche, crush his freedom and suffocate him. He barely stilled a shudder at the threat of such an outcome and thought how ironic it was that what his older brother had longed and prayed for to secure the line to the throne should strike Jasim as an absolute disaster....

* * *

What will proud Prince Jasim do if Elinor is expecting his royal baby? Perhaps an arranged marriage is the only solution! But will Elinor agree? Find out in DESERT PRINCE, BRIDE OF INNOCENCE by Lynne Graham [#2884], available from Harlequin Presents® in January 2010.

REQUEST YOUR FREE BOOKS!

2 FREE NOVELS PLUS 2 FREE GIFTS!

HARLEQUIN®

Blaze™

Red-hot reads!

YES! Please send me 2 FREE Harlequin® Blaze™ novels and my 2 FREE gifts (gifts are worth about $10). After receiving them, if I don't wish to receive any more books, I can return the shipping statement marked "cancel". If I don't cancel, I will receive 6 brand-new novels every month and be billed just $4.24 per book in the U.S. or $4.71 per book in Canada. That's a savings of 15% off the cover price. It's quite a bargain. Shipping and handling is just 50¢ per book.* I understand that accepting the 2 free books and gifts places me under no obligation to buy anything. I can always return a shipment and cancel at any time. Even if I never buy another book, the two free books and gifts are mine to keep forever.

151 HDN EYS2 351 HDN EYTE

Name _____ (PLEASE PRINT)

Address _____ Apt. #

City _____ State/Prov. _____ Zip/Postal Code

Signature (if under 18, a parent or guardian must sign)

Mail to the Harlequin Reader Service:
IN U.S.A.: P.O. Box 1867, Buffalo, NY 14240-1867
IN CANADA: P.O. Box 609, Fort Erie, Ontario L2A 5X3

Not valid to current subscribers of Harlequin Blaze books.

Want to try two free books from another line?
Call 1-800-873-8635 or visit www.morefreebooks.com.

* Terms and prices subject to change without notice. Prices do not include applicable taxes. N.Y. residents add applicable sales tax. Canadian residents will be charged applicable provincial taxes and GST. Offer not valid in Quebec. This offer is limited to one order per household. All orders subject to approval. Credit or debit balances in a customer's account(s) may be offset by any other outstanding balance owed by or to the customer. Please allow 4 to 6 weeks for delivery. Offer available while quantities last.

Your Privacy: Harlequin Books is committed to protecting your privacy. Our Privacy Policy is available online at www.eHarlequin.com or upon request from the Reader Service. From time to time we make our lists of customers available to reputable third parties who may have a product or service of interest to you. If you would prefer we not share your name and address, please check here. ☐

HB09R3

New Year, New Man!

For the perfect New Year's punch,
blend the following:

- One woman determined to find her inner vixen
- A notorious—and notoriously hot!—playboy
- A provocative New Year's Eve bash
- An impulsive kiss that leads to a night of explosive passion!

When the clock hits midnight Claire Daniels
kisses the guy standing closest to her, but
the kiss doesn't end after the bells stop ringing....

Look for

Moonstruck

by *USA TODAY* bestselling author

JULIE KENNER

Available January

red-hot reads

www.eHarlequin.com

HB79518

COMING NEXT MONTH

Available December 29, 2009

#513 BLAZING BEDTIME STORIES, VOLUME III Tori Carrington and Tawny Weber
Bedtime Stories

What better way to spend an evening than cuddling up with your better half, indulging in supersexy fairy tales? We guarantee that sleeping will be the last thing on your mind!

#514 MOONSTRUCK Julie Kenner

Claire Daniels is determined to get her old boyfriend back. She's tired of being manless, especially during the holidays, and she'd like nothing more than a New Year's Eve kiss to start the year off right. And she gets just that. Too bad it's not her ex-boyfriend she's kissing…

#515 MIDNIGHT RESOLUTIONS Kathleen O'Reilly
Where You Least Expect It

A sudden, special kiss between two strangers in Times Square on New Year's Eve turns unforgettable, and soon Rose Hildebrande and Ian Cumberland's sexy affair is smokin' hot despite the frosty weather. Will things cool off, though, once the holiday season ends?

#516 SEXY MS. TAKES Jo Leigh
Encounters

It's New Year's Eve in Manhattan and the ball is about to drop in Times Square…. Bella, Willow and Maggie are on their way to the same blockbuster Broadway audition until fate—and three very sexy men—sideline their journey with sizzling results!

#517 HER SECRET FLING Sarah Mayberry

Don't dip your pen in the office ink. Good advice for rookie columnist Poppy Birmingham. Too bad coworker Jake Stevens isn't listening. Their recent road trip has turned things from antagonistic to hedonistic! He wants to keep this fling on the down-low…but with heat this intense, that's almost impossible.

#518 HIS FINAL SEDUCTION Lori Wilde

Signing up for an erotic fantasy vacation was Jorgina Gerard's ticket to reinventing herself. The staid accountant was more than ready for a change, but has she taken on too much when she meets and seduces the hot, very gorgeous every-woman-would-want-him Quint Mason? She's looking forward to finding out!